THE YAWNING GIANT

A SLIDING DOORS FOOTBALL TALE

MARK BOWMAN

THE YAWNING GIANT
A SLIDING DOORS FOOTBALL TALE

MARK BOWMAN

First published in 2023 by Popcorn Press, an imprint of Fair Play Publishing
PO Box 4101, Balgowlah Heights, NSW 2093, Australia
www.popcornpress.com.au

ISBN: 978-1-925914-71-9
ISBN: 978-1-925914-72-6 (ePub)
© Mark Bowman 2023

Cover illustration by Anastasiia Osypova
Cover design and typesetting by Ana Secivanović

All inquiries should be made to the Publisher via sales@fairplaypublishing.com.au

A catalogue record of this book is available from the National Library of Australia.

DEDICATION

For all passionate football people, past and present,
who want nothing more than the beautiful game
to succeed in Australia

For family and friends

But above all else,
for my late father Harry

CONTENTS

Preface

Sydney, Australia,

September 2022

"The door of history turns on small hinges, and so do people's lives"
—*Thomas S Monson.*

This story is a 'what if' about football in Australia and the National Soccer League in particular.

I call it a 'sliding doors' fiction from the 1998 film by the same name. I also derive inspiration from alternative futures like Philip Dick's *The Man in the High Castle* or my medical colleague David Kowalski's *The Company of the Dead*. If that genre interests you, I highly recommend both novels.

The sliding doors moment in this book occurs on probably the most disastrous night of Australian soccer's long and chequered history—at the Melbourne Cricket Ground during the World Cup qualifier between Australia and Iran in 1997. Australia's failure to see off Iran, and in doing so its failure to qualify for the World Cup held in France in 1998, was devastating not only for the players and the sport but also for the many thousands of football fans across the country—especially those like myself who were there. For many, the mere thought of that game continues to haunt us.

Some readers may have been too young to have experienced the tragedy of that evening, or are more recent to Australian football, so for as many as possible to fully appreciate this novel, that night serves as a preface to this alternative future.

In late 1997, Australia was on the cusp of qualifying for the World Cup after a 24-year absence. FIFA's disdain towards Oceania (the confederation that Australia was then a member of) meant a starvation of true international football until qualification time came around every four years. Then, Australia would see off minnow Pacific nations and (often) New Zealand before being faced with a sudden death home-and-away fixture of a highly ranked team for a place at soccer's biggest stage. After their most improbable and extremely impressive inaugural appearance in 1974 with a talented but amateur side, the Socceroos had stumbled against Iran, New Zealand, Scotland, Israel and Argentina respectively in the subsequent quarter of a century.

For the 1998 World Cup, FIFA deemed that Australia's home-and-away final hurdle would be against the fourth-best Asian team, confirmed to be Iran. The away game came first, a tough-as-nails fixture in Iran's true fortress—the Azadi Stadium in Tehran—replete with 100,000-plus male-only fans all loudly and aggressively willing the Socceroos their worst. The Australians were mighty in that game, escaping with a 1–1 draw, with Australia's goal scored by 19-year-old Harry Kewell.

The return game a few days later was set for Melbourne, at the MCG. A full house, a pre-match motor cavalcade of 1974 Socceroos—finally acknowledged after so many years—and arguably the loudest rendition of 'Advance Australia Fair' in our country's history greeted the players. After kick-off, the game was so one-sided in Australia's favour that in the stands, we were mentally booking our flights to

France within 30 minutes. Australia had wave after wave of attack—with nothing in reply from the Iranians—but frustratingly the Socceroos failed to convert their chances. Finally, in the 32nd minute, Harry Kewell latched on to a cross and sent Australia into the lead. The roof of the MCG was virtually lifted off by the noise.

In the second half, it was more of the same. In the 48th minute, following a superb cross from Stan Lazaridis, Kewell headed back across goal, Craig Foster hit the crossbar, the rebound fell to Aurelio Vidmar who slammed the ball into the roof of the Iranian net. 2–0!!

At this stage, the entire stadium crowd, and the Australian nation currently creating a television rating record watching the game on SBS across the country, were nearly apoplectic.

But at that moment, something curious happened. A man dubbed a serial event pest, Peter Hore, who had already disrupted other sporting events such as the recent Melbourne Cup (for no apparent reason), was also at the game. He jumped the fence and tore the net of the Iranian goal down.

It took eight minutes to repair the net and get the game underway.

It has been the subject of much debate as to whether that act of vandalism was the true cause of what followed. Some argue that the tactical choices and substitutions of Australian coach Terry Venables were at fault. Many, myself included, view that long stoppage as giving the Iranians time to regroup and recharge against the onslaught. In the final 20 minutes of the match, Iran scored twice, and the game finished 2–2.

The home-and-away tie was level at 3–3, but under the away goals rule, Iran qualified. Australia was out of the World Cup yet again.

It was truly a sporting disaster, often described as Australian soccer's Gallipoli, and what followed was a slow and steady decline of particularly the National Soccer League, which folded in 2004.

For many, the rebirth of football in Australia under Frank Lowy healed the wounds. This saw the launch of the A-League, Australia moving from Oceania to the Asian Football Confederation, and the Socceroos' eventual return to the World Cup in 2006 after their incredible defeat of Uruguay. Indeed, many felt that without that elimination in 1997 and the demise of the NSL, the glorious 'new football' would never have eventuated, and Australian soccer would have remained in the doldrums. But despite the successes under Lowy's leadership, there were also failures, one of which was a deepening divide between traditional club football and the franchises that comprised the A-League. This was dubbed by Lowy's first CEO, John O'Neill, as "old soccer" and "new football" as a marketing mantra.

However, as I complete this eight years on from Australia's Asian Cup win in Sydney, and despite the Socceroos' better-than-expected performance at the 2022 World Cup, the A-League is having a crisis of confidence. It is struggling for media attention and crowds, and is suffering with a yet-to-be-proven new television broadcast future. The divisions between 'old soccer' and 'new football' remain and time has healed nothing.

Which has made me think. What might have happened if there had been a different outcome in November 1997? What if the door of history had swung differently on those tiny hinges?

Hence this whimsical work of fiction.

While I've taken the liberty of using the names of real people for this work in most instances in a case of 'what might have been', what follows as part of the story is of course entirely sprung from my mind. Thanks to everyone mentioned and their families in advance for being good sports! Long-term followers of Australian football will instantly recognise most of the characters. Even so, a quick internet search might give context as to their alternative personas. For those new to the game, I hope it will add to your enjoyment of the book to know something about their backgrounds.

And like all things football, there will no doubt be the inevitable debate and disagreement as to where my sliding doors tale has taken Australian soccer. Remember, it's only *one* story—you are entitled to your alternative.

So, with all that in mind, let's return to Melbourne in late 1997...

Chapter 1

Melbourne, Australia,

November 1997

Dave Allenson was a Tigers man through and through. His father had started taking him to Richmond games when he could barely walk and his happiest memories were strolling down Punt Road with his dad, the thrill of crossing the park and entering the Melbourne Cricket Ground, waving his flag and getting to have a meat pie at half time.

He could only just remember the Richmond victories in the 1960s, but the ones in the '70s were more poignant. The happy memories were tainted. During his teenage years he had become more and more aware of his father's drinking and the arguments between his parents late at night. Ultimately it had dawned on him that the unexpected noises associated with their arguing was his father striking his mother. By the time he was 15, his mother had packed the two of them up and walked out.

Life had been tough, with Mum supporting the two of them through cleaning jobs. Dave had struggled through the rest of adolescence and in the end, he had been glad to leave both school and home. A number of labouring jobs had followed as Dave had stumbled, fearful, defensive and unprepared, into adulthood.

Women in particular just hadn't seemed to understand him or his frequent outbursts. A string of failed relationships and relative poverty had sharpened his anger at the world, but it hadn't dented his love for Aussie Rules. He still went to every home game with his mates when not on shift. It had been 17 years since the Tigers had won a flag, but no matter.

Since then, gradually, Dave had gained a better foothold in life. He managed to hold down the rent on a respectable one-bedroom place in South Melbourne and get regular work as a security guard at sporting events. The part-time nature of the job meant regular time at the gym and he was a formidable sight, both in a dark alley and to any streaker at the cricket!

Dave's regular jobs, usually as an on-ground guard, meant he had a bird's-eye view at many of Melbourne's greatest sporting days. He had officiated at a number of grand finals (sadly none involving Richmond), at Boxing Day cricket Tests and at one-dayers. It was, to his mind, a fantastic perk. Hardly even work, given the few times he actually had to do anything. And the MCG was his specialty.

He was less than pleased, however, when his boss, Jim, rang him over his next job.

"What??" he cried down the phone. "Soccer?! At the MCG? What the hell? No one will go! What's the point?"

"They reckon it will be a sell-out, Dave," replied Jim.

"Bullshit!" he snapped back. "And why Iran? Why can't they play a proper sporting country like England? That might actually help their game for once."

There was a long pause, enough time for Jim to get in an audible sigh. "Allenson, do you want the job or not?"

"Of course I want the job. Send me the details," Dave grumbled, then hung up.

Dave's work between the end of the footy season and the international cricket calendar was usually lean. Rent was due next week and quite frankly, he needed the money.

***

November 29, 1997

Fans had been assembling the entire day, both locally and having flown in from around the country. Given the nature of the four-year World Cup cycle and Australia's place in the Oceania Football Confederation leading to a dearth of real fixtures in between, a tradition had emerged that could be traced back a quarter of a century. It was the celebration and passionate support of THE most important international fixture in the quadrennial cycle. For 24 years, it had always ended in glorious failure. But this time, given the opposition and that Australia had come away with not only a draw in Tehran but with a precious away goal, there was greater than usual confidence.

The punters, nearly 100,000 of them, were buoyant. All watering holes within five kilometres of the MCG were overflowing onto the streets, the fans adorned in green and gold, singing and chanting. Then, as kick-off time drew closer, they descended in their masses upon the traditional cricket and footy monolith. The grand old lady of Australian sport had never seen anything like it.

Jim was right about one thing, Dave had to acknowledge as he glanced around the ground just before kick-off. It was *chockers*. There'd been a parade of former players (none of whom he knew) that had been wildly received by the fans, followed by the loudest and most passionate rendition of 'Advance Australia Fair' that he had ever heard. He was emotionally lifted by the sights and the frankly wall of sound that seemed to go straight through him.

Following kick-off though, Dave's disdain of soccer quickly returned. Australia seemed to have endless opportunities to score but could not put the ball in the net. The Socceroos were making raid after raid upon the Iranian goal, particularly down the wings, but somehow that last touch never quite met its mark. The noise and emotion of the crowd was rising and rising by the minute. Dave, behind the goal at the other end of the ground, took it all in. *Typical*, he thought to himself. *This game never has any goals. If we don't score soon, we will have a riot on our hands.*

Dave was one of those characters who held the firm view that soccer violence was a direct result of little scoring, and that the situation could be vastly improved by simply making the goals bigger.

Finally, after about half an hour, the one player Dave had heard of, the young kid Kewell, suddenly scored. The MCG erupted! The forward Vidmar had evaded his defender and sent the ball across the goal mouth to be lashed home by the youngster. Harry Kewell had raced away to the sideline and leant back like a victorious javelin thrower waving his outstretched hand to the crowd, who were by now delirious with excitement.

Dave felt the roof of the stadium would be blown off by the noise. He looked around his section and whilst there was wild cheering and jumping around in the stands, there was no actual trouble that he could see amongst the thousands of bodies and arms waving Australian flags and scarves.

The game continued at a frenetic, one-sided pace. Dave was grateful when half time arrived and hoped that the break might calm the joint.

Hoped being the operative word.

The second half opened, and Dave realised he would have no relief. On the pitch it was more of the same, Australia with heaps of chances, but this time, the crowd didn't have long to wait. The ball came down the left wing, was sent across—again to the young kid on the far post, who headed the ball back across the goal—and like a pinball, was headed again onto the goalpost. The number 10 Vidmar leapt onto the rebound and smashed it home! 2–0!!

Now the crowd went completely crazy. Dave glanced around and noticed his mate Con, patrolling the other side of the behind-goal area, also going nuts and paying no attention to the crowd in front of him.

Shit, Con, do your job! Dave thought momentarily, but as he looked over he saw something far more worrying.

Someone had jumped the fence, not five metres from Con, who hadn't noticed him at all. He had a familiar appearance about him, but all Dave noticed was that he looked like some kind of scruffy hippie with long, scraggly hair and a weird look on his face. In any event, he was heading straight for the goal net!

Con was still oblivious, and Dave realised that it would be down to him to sort this. The hippie was about 15 metres from the goal net and Dave more than 25. To make matters worse, there was an advertising hoarding immediately behind the goal. It would be touch and go.

The hippie went round the hoarding and Dave decided to leap it. That gained him considerable distance. Still, it would be close.

Dave was now three metres from him, the hippie about to grab the net. Dave launched himself and crash-tackled Peter Hore to the ground just in time, sending him sprawling, winded and momentarily unconscious onto the hallowed turf.

Hore, lying prostrate on the ground, came to and gingerly shook his head. Dave towered over the clearly badly injured man, with white rage in his eyes and clenched fists. He was ready to kill him if need be.

"FUCKING SOCCER HOOLIGANS!!!" he screamed. He took a few heaving deep breaths and stormed off, leaving the intruder to the attention of the ambulance officers and police.

Not that most of the crowd noticed, in all the excitement of the goal. Nor the Socceroos who, following wild celebrations, had returned to the halfway line to await kick-off.

***

The game continued. Iran were in complete disarray. It was as if they had no time to breathe, let alone collect their thoughts and play organised football. Somewhere in the pandemonium, Mark Viduka added a third, and the rest of the game was lost in wave after wave of 100,000 people singing choruses of 'Waltzing Matilda', the national anthem and good old-fashioned 'Ole, Ole, Ole' at maximum volume.

Full time came to a raucous atmosphere and a 24-year World Cup drought was broken. Melbourne had never seen a night like it, neither in the ground nor in the all-night partying across the city that was to come. The entire night was seen through with singing and dancing in the streets, and cars with horns blaring and tearing up and down Lygon Street and at multiple other venues until well after dawn.

In the SBS Television commentary booth high above the field, Les Murray and Johnny Warren signed off, put their microphones down, poured themselves each a Scotch and lit up their cigarettes. The on-field post-match interviews lasted for well over 30 minutes and finally the producer, mindful of the history of the occasion but nonetheless acutely aware that they had run well over time, called for the wind-up. Les and Johnny were exhausted and barely held it together during their closing summary. Johnny's final, choked words, captured live on television and remembered forever by the nation, went something like "I'm just so happy for the boys …" Unable to speak more through tears of joy, he simply waved his hand at the camera.

There was a long pause as the first Scotch went down and the first cigarette was nearly finished. "Well, Oreg," said Les at last to his long-term friend, using his favourite nickname. "How was that! It's a new era! The game can only go forward! Can we ever top that?"

"I hope so. I hope so."

Johnny Warren, the famous Socceroo and the most recognisable face of the game in the country, the man who for many best straddled traditional and multicultural Australia from a football perspective, was suddenly introspective. He looked down at his cigarette and stubbed it out. "That's the last one I'm ever having. I want to live long enough to see this through, Lazlo."

"Ha! We'll see how long that lasts!" Les quipped. The two of them downed their second Scotch and went out into the night to join the celebrations.

***

Dave Allenson arrived home late, emotionally and physically exhausted by the long day and high stakes, but internally satisfied that he had stopped a pitch invasion in its tracks. Not that the stupid game of soccer deserved it.

Think I'll stick to footy and the cricket for future work, was the last thing that went through his mind before sleep came.

Chapter 2

Lyon, France,

June 1998

It was 34 degrees Celsius in the blaring sunshine, far too hot for an 'old bloke' to be doing sprints.

Not that Graham Arnold was going to let on to anyone, especially not to Raul Blanco, who was casting a watchful eye over his charges on behalf of the gaffer.

And really, Arnold wasn't worried at all. He might have been nearing 35 years old, but he was as happy as a pig in the proverbial, at the zenith of his long and famous career.

It was a career that had begun with promise shown as a youngster in the Sutherland Shire of Sydney but was clear for all to see by the mid-1980s when he was the national league's top scorer with Sydney Croatia. His call up to the national squad mirrored his success at club level. The stats didn't quite perfectly reflect his nickname at the time, but 'goal-a-game Arnie' had a nice ring to it. An unabashed patriot, the riotous scenes from the dressing room after Australia's historic defeat of Argentina ten years prior in the Bicentennial Gold Cup in Sydney (including his famous line "better get me an ambulance to get me home!") best summed up his character.

A move overseas in 1990 had followed, where Arnold had plied his trade in Belgium and Holland until just the year before. He had played for two clubs, Roda and NAC Breda, in Holland's Eredivisie and had become a local hero for the latter club. *Something that came in very handy a few days ago,* he mused.

Of late he had been in Japan, and whatever was to happen in the next two weeks, he was set for a triumphant return to Australia to head up the newly created Northern Spirit FC.

Beyond that, he thought as he turned for his last sprint, *who knows?* An interest in coaching had started to form in his mind.

He finished the last sprint and took in some big ones to replenish the oxygen debt. *Let's focus on now and enjoy this. The majority of players never get to experience this, after all.*

The training staff had begun to set up for some small-sided games, with the squad taking up their allotted teams and positions.

***

The last seven months had been an absolute whirlwind. After getting on the pitch for the Iran game and experiencing first-hand the sheer exhilaration of qualification after so long, Arnold was determined to maintain his place in the Socceroos squad. Despite the youthful brilliance of Kewell and Viduka (*God they are so good ... so good!*), he knew that the squad would need a more senior forward with experience and nous. If becoming a super sub meant taking part in the world's greatest tournament, so be it.

Almost straight after Melbourne, Australia had a date at the Confederations Cup in Saudi Arabia. After the Iran victory, the Socceroos were flying high. They reached the semi-finals, only to be knocked out just before the final by what Arnold considered to be a very lucky Uruguay. He returned to Japan, worked bloody hard and punched the air when the provisional 26-man World Cup squad, complete with his name, was announced in April. He hot-footed it home for a farewell game in Sydney against—ironically—fellow qualifiers Japan in front of a full house, to be followed by a month-long preparation in Europe leading into the World Cup itself.

That was when the fun really started, largely thanks to the coup that David Hill, the Chair of Soccer Australia, had staged in late 1996 when he secured the services of Englishman Terry Venables as manager of Australia. Only months before taking the Australian job, Venables had managed England at Euro '96 on home soil, losing to Germany on penalties.

Accustomed to being pilloried about all things in his control at Soccer Australia, through qualification Hill had got his own back on his naysayers in the Australian football community at an unimaginable level. Any medium-term threat to his position had been extinguished.

Foreign coaches of developing football nations—as Australia was considered—had the disadvantage of not knowing their charges, but they made up for it through their tactical nous and also their profile with the strings they could pull. 'El Tel' Venables was no different. He was in his element when the squad hit Europe and the British media couldn't get enough of him. Some of it was downright cringeworthy (the XXXX Beer television advertisement was a notable example), but when he said things like "Australia are good enough to win it, you know", the tabloids gave it back page oxygen.

And when he knocked on the door of English FA headquarters, he got a hearing.

The result? The Socceroos' final warm-up friendly would be against England at Wembley, one week out from France '98. The Australian public went wild, the English fans snorted in disbelief.

If the England squad thought that a warm-up against the amateurs from Australia would be the best tonic to prep themselves for France, to further pick themselves up after that harrowing penalty shootout at the same venue two years before, they were sadly mistaken. Despite dominance by the home team for large sections of the match—and a superb 28-minute strike by Alan Shearer, giving England a 1–0 lead at the break—the second half saw the Australians settle more and more into the game as their nerves diminished and their confidence grew. The English and their fans later claimed it was nothing more than the multiple substitutions in the second half. But on 64 minutes, when Harry Kewell had deftly evaded two defenders and slotted the ball past David Seaman, there was unease in the England team and disquiet on the terraces. It was outright anger that swept the ground when on 85 minutes, Viduka received, with his back to goal, a ball from Arnold himself—who had earlier replaced Aurelio Vidmar—and characteristically kept his marker at bay as he turned and put the ball in the top corner of the net. The small contingent of Australian fans, cooped up behind the same goal, went ballistic.

At full time, confirming not only Australia's first football victory over their fiercest sporting rival, but additionally in their first ever meeting on English soil, Arnold thought to himself *they're never going to agree to play us again*, with more than a chuckle.

It was the next morning that the final 22-man squad for France was announced. Graham allowed himself a sly beer that night when he knew that rather than heading home, it was next stop Paris.

***

Australia's group, determined seven months earlier by the official draw, had pitted the Socceroos with Germany, USA, and a squad from Serbia and Montenegro playing under a banner of the Federal Republic of Yugoslavia.

The local, soccer-naïve press already had Australia in second place, but the squad and the football savvy in Australia knew it would be folly to make any assumptions. Football across the planet was rapidly expanding beyond the strongholds of Europe and South America, which meant even the Americans were a threat.

Interestingly, the great post-war migration that had directly led to the emerging Aussie generation spearheaded by the likes of Viduka and Kewell also led to some curious strategic advantages, especially over Yugoslavia. The Socceroos had, in their squad and the community back home, some direct intelligence—none more so than in Australia's brilliant defender Milan Ivanović, a veteran of topflight Yugoslav football through his days with Red Star Belgrade. On top of that, years of war and the break-up of the nation had left Yugoslavia a weakened rump. Croatia was also at the tournament, playing at their first World Cup as an independent nation.

***

After the long build-up, the extensive travelling and the media hype, the Australian contingent were happy to finally be in camp in Lyon and were raring to go for their first match against Yugoslavia, only an hour's drive away at Saint-Etienne.

As they walked onto the pitch, they were greeted by upwards of 10,000 Aussie fans, many of whom had made the long trip from Down Under and bolstered by a fair contingent of European-based expatriates. The fact that they had greater support from the terraces 20,000 kilometres from home as they had for many home games against Oceanic competitors was not lost on the commentators.

Arnold watched intently from the bench as the game quickly became a defensive stalemate. With a match against Germany to come for both teams, neither wanted a loss. The Yugoslavs were well organised in defence, yet matched by Ivanović, supporting his captain Alex Tobin in marshalling the Australian back line. But there was ever present danger, the Yugoslav midfield dominated by the brilliant Dragan Stojković. Despite advancing years and now seeing his club football out in Japan, the nation's captain could create something out of nothing, including playing his compatriot Mijatović through on goal at a moment's notice.

Recognising this from the outset, Venables' game plan was always the use of Australia's greatest asset—their talent and speed down the wings. However, they saw little action during the first half as the players walked to their respective dressing rooms with a goalless half-time score.

The half-time talk had a greater impact on the Socceroos, and they began to use the width of the park more freely. In the 50th minute, Robbie Slater took off down the right wing and sent a looping cross into the box that wasn't dealt with well by the Yugoslav defence. The keeper parried, followed by a mistimed attempted clearance and pinball in the six-yard box as Aurelio Vidmar was on hand to side-foot a bobbling ball home from only a metre out. It wasn't spectacular, ironically so as it would forever go down as the nation's first ever World Cup goal, but nobody in gold cared as the Socceroos went 1–0 up.

Incredibly, it stayed that way! But not before some spirited Yugoslav fightback and some anxious moments in the Aussie defence, including a shot from Stojković from 22 metres out that curled, dipped and hit the left upright before skidding behind for a goal kick. The Australian goalkeeper Mark Bosnich could only watch as the ball flew past him towards its target.

The full-time whistle blew and Australia had their first ever three pointer at the finals. The world's media reacted partly with faint praise and partly with condescension about a plucky underdog effort. The fans on French soil had several hours of celebration ahead of them and those back home watching on their screens had to ready themselves for a tired but joyful day at work after a long and nerve-wracking night. The Socceroos themselves, however, were quickly placed into cotton wool and whisked back to their training base.

More serious stuff was yet to come, but for the first time in their history, it seemed that the Australian football team had finally and properly arrived.

***

If the first match had been a watershed moment for Australia, the second game six days later in Lens was more humbling. This was despite, thanks to Robbie Slater's five-year spell for the local club and marrying a local, having the entire city behind them. Three-time champions Germany were too good for the Socceroos and in a mirror image to their match in Hamburg 24 years previously, defeated the Australians 3–0. The Germans had done their homework, especially on the young forwards Kewell and Viduka. But equally it was clear that the expertise and experience of Milan Ivanović, who had started on the bench for this outing, would be necessary for every game alongside Alex Tobin and not just against his former countrymen.

Nonetheless, the group was very much alive for Australia. Yugoslavia had defeated the United States, who had yet to register a point after a first up defeat by Germany. A win over the Americans would guarantee the Socceroos a round-of-16 place. They held their destiny in their own hands.

There was little turnaround time—only four days—for important work on the training pitch in preparation for the most crucial game in the country's history. Graham Arnold had heard that description put about by the Australian press and laughed. Just about every game in the last seven months had been called "the most important and crucial". The truth was that this team were writing history at a pace of knots. *Long may it continue!* thought Arnold.

Despite the meeting between so-called 'new world' football nations, the stadium was close to full. The Australian fan contingent was growing and clearly outnumbered those of their counterparts. Although they had hosted a successful World Cup only four years before, much more work was required to embed the round ball code into the hearts and minds of everyday Americans. The two countries' federations could learn a lot from each other.

On the pitch, however, there would be no kumbaya in Nantes. At times, the play wasn't pretty, particularly in defence at both ends, with another up-and-coming young player, 21-year-old Craig Moore, the nominated enforcer on the ageing Roy Regerle and equally, Alexi Lalas and Mike Burns taking care of Kewell and Viduka. But gradually the Australian midfield won out, with Ned Zelic and Craig Foster in particular controlling the centre of the park, moving between the American lines more easily. The first goal on 29 minutes came from a beautifully weighted ball by Zelic wide to Lazaridis, sending a low cross to Viduka who controlled with his right foot, shifted the ball to his left, and drove home low from 15 metres.

The Australians knew it wouldn't be enough, and the game tightened in the second half. Nerves were finally settled on 74 minutes, before Viduka struck again in what was to be his final contribution before substitution.

At full time, the entire Socceroos squad ran over to their massive group of supporters for a joint celebration as their next match was announced to all over the loudspeakers.

Their opponents were to come from Group B which had been tight but there was little surprise as to the eventual winner: The Netherlands. The Australian caravan was still on tour. Next stop: Toulouse.

***

The next few days passed quickly. *Now*, Arnold thought, *things are really getting serious*. The Dutch outfit had serious pedigree, including the de Boer brothers, Patrick Kluivert, Edgar Davids, and more seasoned players in Dennis Bergkamp and Wim Jonk. Arnie had played against a number of them at various stages of their careers. Many commentators had chalked them up as title contenders, although others wondered if they were more of a team of individual self-interested champions than a champion team. There was a history of unsettled Dutch squads, after all.

Venables had worked on this in their strategic sessions. "Stay focused, stay calm, stay in their face. If we can get them annoyed with each other, they'll be there for the taking."

If only it were that simple. The Australians were stretched from pillar to post in the first 20 minutes. Only some brave—and lucky— rear-guard action kept the game scoreless.

But by the half-hour mark, the Socceroos were holding their own, with their characteristic wing play coming to the fore.

In the 38th minute, Bergkamp released a thunderous drive from 26 metres that Bosnich tipped around his left upright. At the other end, there were no real clear chances, but the Australians kept the game up to the Dutch and the teams went to the sheds 0–0 at half time.

After the break, the Aussie midfield started to come into their own.

A couple of intercepted Dutch passes, some penetration between the lines, and Foster was away on goal. He was bundled over by Frank de Boer just outside the box. Moore moved up to take the free kick but sent the ball a metre over the crossbar.

From there, the Dutch got a little riled. They no longer enjoyed midfield control. More stray passes were followed by a few hopeful longer balls. A combination of frustration and formation breakdown ensued and, suddenly, Bosnich had little to do.

With 18 minutes to go, the call came across the bench. "Arnie! Warm up!" Five minutes later, his number was being held up to replace Aurelio. He was brought into the game and, Graham Arnold realised, into history. If things didn't change in the next 14 minutes, he was part of extra time and everything else that came with it.

Full time. No goals.

Extra time seemed to come and go in a flash, but a combination of tiredness, cramps and Dutch ill-discipline prevented any decent goal-scoring opportunities. At 120 minutes, the teams couldn't be separated.

The game moved to penalties.

The Australians were exhausted but, just as they had at full time, they stayed on their feet. They weren't about to give anything away to the Dutch. The outfielders were in a huddle, with Blanco reiterating the agreed list and order of penalty takers. Arnold knew his turn and his strategy, but his mind had quickly turned to the videos his friends in Holland still sent to him every week following his move to Japan. The Australian management would have little knowledge of the young sub Boudewijn Zenden from PSV Eindhoven, but Arnie remembered two recent shootouts in the Dutch Cup.

Mark Bosnich was three metres away with the goalkeeping coach, simultaneously looking around and listening to instructions. Arnold looked up from the huddle and across to him.

"Boz! BOZ!!" He got the keeper's attention. "Zenden! He goes left! Your right! Every time!"

Bosnich's demeanour suddenly shifted to one of intense focus and clarity. He stared seriously and deeply into Graham Arnold's eyes for what seemed like an eternity, before grinning broadly and giving Arnie a thumbs up.

Holland, going first, converted their first three penalties, but each was responded in kind with cleanly taken efforts by Kewell, Moore and Lazaridis.

The Netherlands' fourth was put away by Kluivert, and Arnie was next. It had already dawned on him that the Dutch keeper would know a lot about him but over the years Arnie had shot to both sides in different matches.

Arnold's effort, doubtless impacted by nerves, was underhit. It didn't matter. It was on target, and the keeper went the other way. It was 4–4 with a kick to come for each side.

Zenden was next. *Typical Holland*, Arnie thought. *Having enough faith in the young stars to let one take such an important strike.*

Zenden calmy put the ball on the spot. Bosnich crouched, focused and ready. A few steps back, and Zenden hit the ball to the Australian keeper's upper right, but Bosnich was ready for it. He'd started to move the exact instant Zenden struck the ball. Bosnich parried the ball away to safety and, incredibly, the Socceroos were one kick away from the quarter finals of the World Cup.

Up stepped Mark Viduka. Arnold couldn't watch. He'd seen 'Dukes' in training and some of his takes were so-so.

Viduka muttered something to himself in Croatian, ran forward and hit the ball straight down the centre, over the heels of the keeper who had dived left. Almost in slow motion, the ball hit the back of the net.

Viduka turned and held his arms aloft, and then real time returned as he was swamped by the entire Australian squad charging at full pace from the centre circle and the bench.

***

The overly warm training session in Lyon was coming to an end and Graham Arnold's reflections of the past couple of weeks faded as he refocused on the present. As usual, he would stay on for a further hour or so working on set pieces and penalties. He might as well, he thought—he knew that his roommate 'Bulldog' would be in the bathroom for an eternity …

Chapter 3
Marseille, France,

July 1998

It was a four-hour coach ride from their base outside Lyon to their quarter final venue at the Stad Velodrome in Marseille. For good measure, the entire squad had moved two days before and were holed up at a venue they wanted to keep as secret as possible. South American fans had a habit of creating all-night noise outside hotel rooms to tire their opponents.

There was a rumour that Soccer Australia were saving money by using the officially supplied FIFA coach, rather than flying the team to their next venue. In reality, there was probably little difference once the squad travelled to and from each airport, in addition to the flying time itself. Anyway, Stan Lazaridis didn't care. Flying, especially in small aeroplanes in turbulent conditions, scared the shit out of him.

The bus trip had been buoyant, even jubilant. Those that wanted time to themselves had no chance. Alcohol had been banned by Venables but that didn't stop the high spirits and the hijinks. Stan decided that there was no escaping and that the best form of defence was attack, or at least to place himself right at the eye of the storm. He chose to sit next to Mark Bosnich.

In the end, the injury toll only amounted to a few cola-sprayed bodies, a couple of bruised egos and one episode of car sickness. One upside that Lazaridis remembered forever was the brief stop in Montélimar where, on alighting for a quick snack and halfway toilet stop, they were greeted and cheered by thousands of locals. Their escapades to date had endeared them not only to the everyday French, but lovers of the underdog everywhere.

***

Still just 25 years old, Stan Lazaridis occasionally had to pinch himself as to how his football career had turned out. Raised in Perth, he'd been spotted by Harry Redknapp during a West Ham pre-season tour in 1995. His first season at Upton Park had been a bit so-so, but after that he had well and truly cemented his place as an exciting and valuable left winger at the Premier League club. He had even scored a couple of goals for the Hammers in the season just completed. Stan was a no-nonsense type, and his attitude had gelled with the West Ham gaffer, the quintessential Anglo-Saxon football manager, as well as the team's traditional cockney base. It was no surprise that Terry Venables also thought highly of him.

Stan was first choice for the left sided position in the Australian first eleven and had contributed an assist in the first round at *France '98*, in addition to the cross he put on that led to the Socceroos' second goal at the final qualifying match in Melbourne in November.

Many regarded that moment as being the crucial turning point in the long and tortuous history of Australian football.

And now, here he and his countrymen were, about to compete in the quarter finals of the World Cup itself. The 1974 Socceroos had reached 'Base Camp' when they became the first Aussie team to qualify for the

World Cup, but 24 years later, this was unarguably the dizziest heights towards football 'Everest' that the country had experienced.

If only it didn't have to be against that most wily and enigmatic of teams: the team that tossed them aside in qualifying only five years previously—Argentina.

***

The preparations were complete. The squad was at peak fitness; only two suspensions for double yellow cards prevented the strongest possible line-up. The tactics had been drilled in, over and over again.

The team was clearly up for it and the managerial staff had their own motivations. Assistant coach Raul Blanco, a fiercely loyal Australian but Argentine by birth, knew full well the challenge but tried to not let his head rule his heart. As for Venables, in many ways the English coach wanted this more than anyone.

The teams strode out onto the field. Open on three sides, the stands were baking in the heat. But despite that and the fact the tiers sloped only gently, leaving the cheap seats some distance from the game, the Argentine fans were making an incredible noise. A modest contingent of Australians, maybe 10,000 or so, largely tucked into one corner, were doing their best, but they were no match for the fans of the *Albicelestes*.

The official niceties were completed, and the game began in a cagey fashion. Australia were wary of over-commitment in attack lest they get caught out at the back. Nerves were probably playing a role as well, although the players would never have admitted it.

Argentina had done their homework. The defensive midfielder Almeyda had decided Lazaridis was going nowhere without him—not even to the toilet at half time. The left side, so often beneficial for the Socceroos, was largely shut down as Lazaridis was prevented, mostly fairly, from the getting the ball forward.

On 24 minutes, there was an uncommon break from midfield for Australia. Milanović to Foster, forward to Viduka in quick succession, but the resulting shot was just wide of the right upright.

Argentina slowly but surely settled into a game pattern they knew only too well. Skilful footwork and close ball control, gradually connecting their passes, yet interspersed with quickly going to ground when necessary. They would roll and exaggerate any potential injury, along with liberal doses of surrounding the referee with gesticulated protestations.

On 38 minutes, the Argentine right winger sent a wicked curling and dipping cross into the Australian box. The number 9 brought it down brilliantly from knee height, straight to his feet; in an instant he fired home. Bosnich had no chance, Gabriel Batistuta wheeled away to the corner flag and was piled upon by his teammates. 1–0.

Australia were rattled and disjointed, yet somehow they got to half time with just the one goal deficit.

***

The Socceroos entered the dressing room and many slumped into their seats. Venables was calm and clear. "Keep going, you're doing fine. Stick to the game plan, get your passes completed."

Senior squad leaders completed the break with spirited words of encouragement. Renewed, the team made its way back onto the field.

***

The second half became a midfield tussle. There was fairly even possession, but neither side had obvious opportunities to score.

Then, in the 64th minute, there was trouble for Australia. Craig Moore, 20 metres out from goal, brought down Hernan Crespo and was immediately given a yellow card. The wily Argentine forward, a wizard with the ball at his feet, had turned on a dime and left Moore's attempt at the ball instead with stud marks on Crespo's ankle. It wasn't intentional, but it was appropriately punished.

On the bench, Raul Blanco immediately panicked. Well-versed in his birth nation's tricks, he knew what was in store for the final 25 minutes. Any further attempted tackle by Moore would lead to an immediate fall to the turf, trying to incite a red from the official.

However, more immediate danger was at hand. The Argentines had a free kick in a perfect position, just outside the box and left of centre. It was tailor-made for Claudio Lopez to bend a wicked curling kick around the wall and into the Australian net.

Amongst the players and in the stands, the Australian tension was unbearable. Three Argentines were over the ball, all waving wildly at the referee, pointing at the Aussie wall, the goal, anything to disrupt any clear process or plans. The Socceroos' defenders, looking around anxiously, gradually organised themselves while Bosnich screamed at them to form their wall and get themselves into the correct position. The referee demanded the wall move further back to the required yardage, pointedly moving his hand to his pocket should his instructions not be obeyed. With deafening crowd noise, the whole scene was being played out in front of thousands of Argentine supporters behind the net, doing their best to disrupt any semblance of Australian structure.

The whistle went. One Argentine ran at the ball but feigned. The next, Claudio Lopez, struck the ball sweetly. The wall could only watch when, as expected, it flew by them and towards the goal. Top right corner. Bosnich leapt and was beaten, but the upright wasn't. The ball rebounded into play and Ivanović hooked it clear.

The bench exhaled a collective sigh of relief. Blanco turned to Venables. "Sub!" he yelled over the noise. Venables, as usual, had an impassive look on his face. Then Raul realised the dilemma.

Their next experienced defender, Steve Horvat, was suspended after picking up successive yellow cards against Germany and Holland. What to do—risk a red card for Moore or risk bringing on the experienced, but in this tournament squad player only, Robbie Hooker? It was clear from his inaction that El Tel had opted for the former. Internally, Blanco disagreed but was powerless.

The Socceroos battled to keep their shape. They knew that time was running out to get the equaliser. Wing play was their natural fallback tactic, but the *Albicelestes* defenders dealt with the increasing number of high crosses, or even attempted square balls on the deck to the Aussie forwards with ease.

In the 71st minute, the inevitable occurred. Moore won the ball cleanly from his opponent side on, but with some minimal contact leading to Batistuta collapsing to the ground, writhing around in 'pain'. The German referee reached immediately to his pocket and produced a red card.

The Australians surrounded the referee with howls of protest and gesticulations indicating a dive. But as always in this situation, it was to no avail. Moore trudged off and down the tunnel with the look of an innocent man on death row.

Too late, the substitution was made. Hooker for midfield man Foster, rather than a striker, to at least keep some semblance of attack.

But on 85 minutes, the death knell was struck. Simeone to Crespo, a through ball to Batistuta, who rubbed salt into raw Australian wounds by slotting the ball home and initiating wild melodramatic celebrations. 2–0 to Argentina. For the Socceroos, the jig was up.

The final five minutes seemed a blur to Stan Lazaridis who had run his guts out, up and down the left wing for the entire match. When the final whistle came, he just stood, staring across the field with a grimace of devastating acceptance. Many of his teammates collapsed to the ground. Bosnich just sat on the turf, legs splayed, leaning back on his hands.

***

The players were distraught, but in the fullness of time would come to realise what a magnificent World Cup they had, exceeding all expectations and creating their own history in the process. *France '98* would be remembered not only in the local Australian press but around the world, for the local team's first championship, for the newly reborn Croatia's run and for the performance of the 'minnows' from Down Under.

Across Australia, the tournament was viewed as football's coming of age at home.

Books were written about the fans' experiences, the new culture and the bright future—the "time Australia became a football nation".

Above all else, thanks to Moore's sending-off, many commented upon the fact that just like in other countries, Australian punters now had their very own moment of World Cup injustice. That red card was doubtless the unconscious work of officialdom leading to bias, to ensure that only the 'pedigreed' teams get to the pointy end of the World Cup.

The day after their loss, the squad disbanded, some players retired and the coach's unlikely contract ended. For the aeroplane-shy Lazaridis, he was on his way to a much overdue Greek island holiday before his return to London—by ferry.

Chapter 4

Sydney, Australia,

November 2000

The arms and hands that held, then put down, the detailed progress report and accounts were adorned by a perfectly tailored Italian shirt complete with beautiful cufflinks, but their owner's face wore a frown of concern.

Because deep down, Remo Nogarotto knew that—unlike his wardrobe—his business model was full of holes.

It should have been a success story, after all. Created just as Australia had qualified for and exceeded all expectations at the World Cup in France, the Northern Spirit Football Club seemingly had everything going for it. Friday nights at North Sydney Oval had been well attended family-friendly events. Game day had a fun, almost carnival-like feel, prefaced by face painting and sky divers, with good-natured singing and chanting from the Bob Stand behind the north-eastern goal mouth. Much of the crowd consisted of new fans to the NSL and the club represented a geographical area not historically part of the national league landscape. The northern region of Sydney consisted of hundreds of well-resourced community football clubs and a vast number of young and old alike who, despite their traditional affection for rugby union, played, coached and knew soccer. Along with Perth Glory and the Brisbane Strikers, Northern Spirit represented a new face of the league that was truly regional and 'non-ethnic'.

Furthermore, the club's roster consisted of some of Australia's true greats of football, inaugurally by two World Cup heroes and poster boys in Graham Arnold and Robbie Slater. One, a journeyman of world football, had accomplished himself in Belgium, Holland and Japan; the other a French League 1 then English Premier League star with a Blackburn Rovers winner's medal to boot. The squad had also been bolstered by the recent return of Craig Foster from the United Kingdom.

Nogarotto knew the issues and he had depth of experience when it came to the challenges of football administration. A soccer man through and through, at an early age he found himself elevated to the Marconi board with all the trials and tribulations that that had entailed. But the Spirit was his show, and he knew what his financial backers expected.

In short, many of the apparent positives about the club were in fact transpiring to be weaknesses.

The startup squad and the coaching staff were all credentialled, but they had been less than successful on the park. Established teams over the seasons easily accounted for Northern Spirit, especially when they were away from North Sydney Oval. There were guest imports, but too often they enjoyed the prospect of a holiday and the local cuisine rather than the football. The crowds had started to wane.

After all, this was rugby heartland—and the Wallabies were on top of the world, having recently defeated the All Blacks and the British and Irish Lions, topped off by winning the Rugby World Cup only the year before. Soccer was a great game for the kids, but North Shore fathers were rusted onto a different code.

And then there was North Sydney Oval. Its location was perfect; it was an easy drive down Epping Road, the Pacific Highway, across the Roseville Bridge or from Manly in the lower Northern Beaches. The train station was just downhill from the ground. On match evenings, local establishments like the Rag and Famish did a brisk trade with the football punters, leading up to the kick-off. The usual ghost-town evenings in the city of North Sydney were banished, for one night a fortnight at least.

No, the problem wasn't the location of North Sydney Oval, but the ground itself. The complex was a heritage site, beautiful old stands lovingly restored to their former glory. Some, like the Bob Stand, had been moved holus-bolus from the Sydney Cricket Ground, salvaging them from the concrete bowl that much of the SCG was becoming. However, not one of those beautiful stands seemed to bear any relationship to the layout of the football pitch on the ground itself. Most fans ended up with a sore neck from watching the game at a 20-to-30-degree angle to their seats.

Then, of course, there was the pitch itself. Like all great ovals around the country, North Sydney Oval was a cricket field first and foremost, and the large wicket square in the centre of the ground took on a consistency of concrete more than turf. *No wonder we don't have any decent-performing central midfielders*, Remo mused. The players all avoided the cricket square like the plague for fear of injury and regularly sent the ball down the wings instead.

It was the ultimate rectangular peg in an oddly shaped round hole. For a football ground, North Sydney Oval made for a great Historical Society picnic site. It was an insult that the council were charging the club a motza to use it.

Remo knew that they could move from North Sydney Oval, possibly to Manly, but that wouldn't help the crowd numbers. In any event, the council deal was locked in for the season.

No, despite all the challenges besetting Northern Spirit, the greatest of all was beyond the control of the club. Soccer in Australia was in gradual decline. Once again, just like after 1974, it seemed as if the legacy of a World Cup appearance was about to go begging. Although back then, at least it spurned the formation of the NSL— even if it took three years to finally get it off the ground. This time, could it really be that the national league was dying a slow death, despite a performance in France that would be the envy of the vast majority of the football world?

It wasn't for a lack of decent players. The Australian system continued to turn out youngsters who headed off to Europe to ply their trade. Maybe, in fact, that was part of the problem. Apart from the occasional sighting on television, they weren't usually seen until World Cup qualification games. Even then, it was touch and go as to whether their club managers would release them for the long flight home and back, especially for games against minnow Pacific nations in early qualifying stages. Last minute 'injuries' preventing travel were common.

Cable television was starting to show more European football than SBS Television's *The World Game* ever could over the preceding decade. It was increasingly obvious to everyone what most had suspected for years—local football couldn't hold a candle to overseas leagues with respect to style and support.

But it wasn't that bad, thought Remo. *And you can't get the same game-day experience sitting in front of a television.*

No, there was something broader at work. The administration of football was severely lacking in Australia, and it was combined with a greater disinterest, even negative bias, when it came to soccer. From government to the press to business, it was the same. No one was even interested in trying to help the game. The recent Olympics in Sydney was a perfect example. Every other Olympic sport received some sort of legacy, from archery to rowing, except football. Not only had no new facilities for football been developed for *Sydney 2000*, group games that were played interstate were played at *cricket* grounds. What was worse, grounds like the Gabba in Brisbane were upgraded for the privilege, a move that directly benefited Aussie Rules football (AFL) and cricket rather than soccer. *It was a disgrace*, thought Remo.

Sure, he reasoned, the game might never be the number one sport in Australia, but there had to be enough experienced people—administrators, players, fans—who together could form a stable, viable base for the game here? Furthermore, can't the mainstream population and media appreciate and remember what it was like to be part of the world's greatest game? They did only two years ago, after all.

And can't people support more than one sport in this country? The last World Cup showed there was plenty of evidence for traditional AFL fans supporting the Socceroos. They could support both cricket and AFL, why not football into the mix?

Remo had spent the last few months sorting out his financial backers. The original consortium of Malaysian backers had already sold their investment to Crystal Palace owner Mark Goldberg, but he had since run into financial difficulties and indicated a year ago that he wanted to divest himself of the club. Remo had spent many hours of negotiating and convincing new owners to come in and suffered many sleepless nights as a result. He now had a patchwork of investor groups, individual backers and an overdraft holding it all together. Often it felt like a house of cards in a strong breeze.

He glanced again at the accounts and frowned again. *If we don't get radical change, I reckon they'll give me two more seasons,* Remo decided of his new backers.

Chapter 5

Sydney, Australia,

November 2001

The news had come through from South America, just as the final full-time whistles on that continent's last round of qualifiers had sounded.

Paraguay.

Despite a heavy loss to Colombia, a gutsy home win by Uruguay over their fierce rivals Argentina had sealed *La Celeste* as fourth and ensured Paraguay were fifth. As such, they would meet Australia home and away for the final position for *Korea-Japan 2002*.

"That's not so bad, is it? I've not heard of them doing much …" said a junior staffer at Soccer Australia who clearly didn't have a complete grasp of global football.

Ian Holmes, the Federation's general manager, had an older head on his shoulders when it came to logistics and opponents. He pulled the atlas off the shelf and located Paraguay's capital Asuncion. "This is going to be a nightmare," he replied more realistically. "The two games will be about five days apart, doubtless they'll convince FIFA to play in Australia first. We've got to get as many European-based players here in time as we can. Then the squad will have a 15-hour flight to Santiago and a change to their capital Asuncion for what—

another three-hour flight? We've got to find decent flights, decent accommodation for both legs in two weeks' time and we haven't got two bob to rub together in this organisation."

***

Melbourne, Australia, November 2001

Jack Reilly had just hung up the phone, completely exasperated. Really, there was no point getting him on to the Board of Soccer Australia for his expertise if he wasn't going to be listened to, let alone be outvoted.

The Australian '74 World Cup goalkeeper and now successful businessman had the perfect blend of football experience and operational nous to be a huge boon to the activities and potential for Soccer Australia. But his sharp Scottish temperament had come to the fore. It was frustrating to him that yet again, the Federation was reaching for the rifle, determined to shoot itself in the foot.

He had tried to be as succinct as possible. "David, it's important to throw everything at this. Just like you did five years ago by appointing Venables. We're stuck with the home leg first—God knows why we couldn't have argued harder, but I accept that we may never have gotten otherwise. But if we under-resource this, it will blow up in our faces. The squad will need business class flights, efficient transfers with appropriate and high standard accommodation away from noise."

Hill was, as usual, full of reassuring smooth talk. "They'll be fine, Jack. We'll do our best. But we can't afford business class tickets for a 30-man contingent—"

"You could if you hadn't sold the Federation short on that television deal—"

"That has nothing to do with it. They'll cope, they're young, fit professionals. They were quarter finalists at the last World Cup, after all!"

Jack repressed an expletive. "Even the reigning world champions would not do well with 18 hours of flying with their knees under their chins, David, and you damn well know it." He took a breath. "You do realise how important it is for the game that we qualify again, don't you? The average Australian has a short memory, the national league hasn't hit the highs that were expected after France. And most importantly, for once we will have a World Cup next year where all games will be played at decent television viewing times. The Socceroos will be prime time ratings winners."

"I'm well aware of that, Jack. But the board, the majority of whom as you know are here in Sydney, have already determined the plans and budget outlay for the two legs."

Bloody hell, fumed Reilly as he stormed out of his office for some fresh air. *Korea-Japan 2002 would be the Socceroos' biggest chance to cement the game in the minds of the average Aussie sports fan, and odds-on we are going to fuck it up.*

***

Despite its oval shape and massive distance of the actual field of play from the fans, with a surface more attuned to any other sport than football, the Melbourne Cricket Ground had again been chosen to host Australia's most important home fixture in four years. Given the spectacular success of the Iran game, both on and off the pitch, it was a no-brainer.

As usual, the earlier qualifiers had been routine. Apart from seeing off the various Oceania teams that FIFA had slung in front of Australia—with all locally based players—there was the inevitable home-and-away clash with the Kiwis. After their highs nearly two decades ago when they qualified for *Spain '82*, sadly, New Zealand football had undergone a slow and steady decline.

As always, however, the fixtures against New Zealand were tougher in reality than on paper. Having similarly breezed through their early Oceania qualifiers, the New Zealand Football Association decided it was time to really make a statement, especially as they were about to play World Cup quarter finalists—not that they were ready to use those words in public. Overlooking the previously used but rather provincial Mount Smart Stadium and the more modern but agricultural underfoot North Harbour—where they had failed against the Socceroos four years earlier—the NZFA decided to go all out and play the match at the celebrated Eden Park. Upgraded for the first Rugby World Cup final nearly 15 years earlier, it was the go-to ground for the All Blacks but had hosted everything from rugby league tournaments to the 1992 Cricket World Cup.

The venue was chosen to attract as large and a passionate a home crowd as possible. It was hoped to be a counterfoil for the return leg at Stadium Australia in Sydney the following weekend.

Australia were not at full strength for the two-legged tie. Many of their international stars had returned from Europe but there were the notable absences of Harry Kewell and Mark Viduka.

The Kiwis were defensive-minded from the start and, collectively, that meant a rather stale and ultimately goalless affair. Compared with their recent performance at the Confederations Cup, Australia were tepid.

In Sydney, however, it was a different kettle of fish. Early goals by Brett Emerton and John Aloisi overcame any nerves that the Kiwis might nab a precious away goal, and when David Zdrilic added a third on 49 minutes, the rest was fairly pedestrian.

Four months later and the confederation play-off squads had arrived in Melbourne. Australia had, much to the relief of everyone, secured their strongest possible squad but it was the names that the average non-football savvy didn't recognise on the opponent's side that were more impressive. Players like Carlos Gamarra, Celso Ayala and José Cardozo, with José Luis Chilavert in goal behind them, were forging their own reputations in a remarkably similar timeframe to their Aussie opponents. Up front they had their young star and Bayern Munich regular Roque Santa Cruz. The *Albirroja* had been developing their own, in many ways more formidable, golden generation.

Ninety-five thousand packed the MCG on an unseasonably cold and windy late spring evening in Melbourne. If the level of excitement pre-match was similar to four years ago, after kick-off, the mood on the terraces was far more subdued. Paraguay were clearly in a different class to Iran and after 18 rounds of CONMEBOL qualification, were a far more tightknit and battle-hardened group. It was clear that either in Melbourne or Asuncion, there was going to be little way through for the Australian forwards. Ayala's work in particular, whose day job with River Plate was to eat flashy Argentine forwards for breakfast, meant it was a hard day at the office for Kewell and Viduka. Somehow, in the 38th minute, a well-worked midfield move between Paul Okon and Emerton opened up the Paraguay defence and put Kewell through to score! The crowd, aside from the modest South American contingent, were suddenly brought to life from their silenced anxiety. Maybe it would be all right on the night after all.

But the euphoria was short-lived. A wicked curling free kick flashing just past Mark Schwarzer's right post just before half time lowered the mood in the stands. Then, in the second half, it was one-way traffic for the *Albirroja*. It was only a matter of time before the inevitable when on 61 minutes, Cardozo equalised by converting a low powerful and curling cross. In the end, a 1–1 score line was flattering for the Socceroos, and Paraguay had a precious away goal.

And now the fun really starts, thought Jack Reilly, watching from the stands, as the players departed the field for the journey from hell.

***

Asuncion, Paraguay, November 2001
Even if the flights had been torture, the reception and treatment of the Socceroos after their arrival had been first class and gracious. Both squads had been fast-tracked through border protection and the Australians whisked without fuss to their hotel. The training facilities provided were more than adequate and they were even allowed a session at the *Estadio Defensores del Chaco* the day before the game itself.

The Australian coach, Frank Farina, took it all in. *They're not scared of us in the slightest*, he concluded to himself. A contemporary of Arnold and Slater, Farina had retired from international competition in 1995 as a 31-year-old at the peak of his career which had included multiple championships in Australia and Belgium, as well as playing stints in France, Italy and England. Now aged just 37, he had been coach of the Australian team for two years—a choice made by the Soccer Australia Board on the basis of cost rather than experience and qualifications.

Farina was right in his assessment. Come game day, 50,000 rabid locals packed the stadium and witnessed their team control the match from start to finish. Goals in either half from Cardozo and Santa Cruz respectively merely raised the already continuous deafening noise that meant the Australians could barely think, let alone communicate with each other.

The game, and the dream of a third World Cup appearance, were gone in a flash. The enduring image of the Socceroos was an inconsolable and tearful Tony Vidmar being helped off the field by his teammates.

Perhaps Australia's poor administrative planning had made a difference, perhaps it was the order of the two-game tie that in reality was out of their control. More likely it was simply that Paraguay were too good, or a combination of all three. But one thing was certain: it was back to business as usual for Australian soccer. A golden opportunity to cement the game in the hearts and minds of the country, particularly with the upcoming World Cup in Australia's hemisphere, was again wasted.

An administration bereft of ideas and money, stuck in a culture of groups of men with varying degrees of personal success using the game as a warring plaything. A league withering on the vine, with waning crowds and a long track record of horrific financial mismanagement. And a confederation not worthy of direct qualification to the event generally viewed as the local game's only rainmaker.

The punters sighed and shrugged their shoulders. Another quarter of a century of misery seemed likely.

Chapter 6

Across Australia,

December 2002

It was the weekend of round 10 of the 2002–2003 National Soccer League. Across the country, the ever-declining number of Australian soccer tragics were going through the motions. Some with greater optimism than others.

In Adelaide, on a warm Saturday evening, Andrew Howe stood on the terraces of Hindmarsh Stadium with renewed purpose. The match between the newly formed Adelaide United and Perth Glory had been well attended and with ten minutes to go, Adelaide were in the lead despite the Glory's deadly strike force of Damian Mori and Bobby Despotovski.

Howe knew every detail about them, of course. Howe was a statistician by profession and obsessed by numbers. Some years ago, he had combined this with his passion for football, and a 'monster' had been created. He had been busily compiling the statistics of every national league game from its inception nearly 15 years ago. The later rounds were all complete but updating and expanding the ledger for much of the early years still required some work.

Bar some stray Glory fans, like every Adelaide football game since the wind-up of West Adelaide, the evening's match was essentially an all local one-club gate attendance. Howe constantly juggled pride and amazement as to what had transpired in his adopted city over the last few months. After years of political infighting and wrangling, the incumbent Adelaide City had effectively collapsed and a consortium of like-minded businesspeople had created a new team with city-wide representative colours. They presented it to the local populace who across all ages, backgrounds and ethnic groups had snapped it up. The mood and the crowds were buoyant. Over 8,000 were in attendance tonight, although Andrew would of course get the exact number into his database in a couple of days.

To top it off, this was a true city-city clash. *If only we could have another six or seven of these every week across the country,* Howe thought to himself. But he was no mug when it came to football and its politics. He knew it was a different story over east, where many sectarian challenges remained. He had seen it all first-hand, growing up in Sydney and watching teams like APIA and St George-Budapest for many years. With a small group of fans, he would stand on the grassy hill behind the goal and get behind St George, much to the bemusement of the European immigrants in the grandstand.

Full time sounded and it was three points to the locals. Howe left the ground surrounded by a throng of upbeat youngsters. The night was still young, and he decided he would have plenty of time to catch that new heavy metal band downtown.

***

The next day, on Sunday afternoon in Brisbane, David Marshall took his seat in the compact Bill Waddell Stand at Perry Park. A popular general practitioner with spectacular vocabulary, a sharp, quick wit and an offbeat sense of humour, football was his lifelong passion. He enjoyed and understood not only the game, but also its culture and the at times pomposity and silliness that endeared people to football across the planet.

He also understood the woeful administration of Australian soccer and the bias that the local game endured. Born in Salford in England, giving him automatic rights to be a Manchester United supporter, he had grown up in Tasmania. At school, the headmaster had punished him for trying to arrange a soccer competition, being sternly told in no uncertain terms "we only play the Australian game here".

In adulthood, having established himself in Brisbane, his adopted club the Strikers generally had mixed fortunes over the years and were usually short of the mark. Their grand final win of 1997 was by far and away the high watermark, but sadly had not been replicated since. This season, however, was looking more positive. Having been unceremoniously relieved of his duties as national coach following the loss to Paraguay, Frank Farina had returned to coach the Strikers and had assembled a competitive if workman-like team.

David genuinely wanted the Australian game to succeed at both international and club level. He had been behind the goal at the MCG in 1997 and revelled long into the night when World Cup qualification had been achieved again after so long. But in all honesty, it was hard to ever see the game getting anywhere in this new century.

David glanced around the ground. There were likely 1,000 in attendance at best. A far cry from the heady days of five years ago.

He had done his best over the years to drum up support, although friends had goaded him to be more adventurous. "Why don't you offer free medical consultations to all those who in return, agree to attend the next home game?" he had once been facetiously asked on the email chat group Oz Soccer. "It doesn't work," he had replied.

The Strikers had been battling with limited purpose for most of the match and it was only a matter of time before the inevitable. The Knights' front two virtually strolled past the pedestrian defence to make it 1–0 to the visiting team.

Oh well, thought Marshall. It was time to start one of his many preoccupations when the spark was out of the game in front of him. This time it was a version of pass the parcel as a hat containing ten dollars was handed from friend to friend every time an unforced passing error was made by the home team. At the full-time whistle, the holder of the hat kept the cash. It was one of his favourites and, as usual, he was not surprised when the hat did several rotations in the final 20 minutes.

***

That same afternoon in northern Sydney, Geoff Coy and Mike 'Gremlin' Garner pulled up outside the suburban cladded house in Epping to collect the third member of their party for the day. After some brief pleasantries with Mrs Bowman, they settled her husband Harry in the front passenger seat—out of respect—with Gremlin taking the rear seat for the trip down to Belmore Oval. It wasn't often that they went to see Northern Spirit away, but given this was against Olympic, whom Harry had occasionally followed in earlier days of the NSL, they made an exception.

The three had first met in the 1980s when supporting the Socceroos from behind the goal at the northern end of the Sydney Football Stadium. The unofficial collection of supporters, which at times could number well over 100, took their name *Bay 23* from the numbered section of the stand they were in.

The group was an eclectic cross section of society, including students, tradespeople, bankers, accountants, lawyers and doctors. Undoubtedly, many of the English-migrated in the group, who generally adorned themselves with crew cuts and Doc Martens boots, were hoping to relive some of the terrace experience they had left behind in pre-Premier League England. Sadly, with the help of the many die-hard NSL followers in the group, that occasionally spilled over into a bit of bovver for dissenting opposition fans of whichever team Australia was playing. But mostly the banter was good-natured and always began with the ritual consumption of more than a few beers at the nearby Cricketers Arms Hotel in Surry Hills.

Harry was somewhat different in both age and philosophy. He was the son of a Cockney-born fellow of the same name who had left England in the 1920s with his parents and siblings, to resettle in the western Sydney suburb of Auburn in a house suitably renamed 'West Ham'. Despite his adoration of the motherland, Harry Senior in due course instilled in his young son an incredible sense of loyalty and patriotism to Australia—after all, that was where he was born—especially on the sporting field. Combined with an over-developed Anglo-Saxon sense of justice and what was right and wrong, in due course the younger Harry took the wider family's love of football upon himself. He was rusted on for life, for better or worse.

In 1951 Harry had watched England defeat Australia 17–0 at the old Sydney Sports Ground and suffered every time the Aussie keeper Norm Conquest fished the ball out of his net. Harry swore that one day he would live to see soccer succeed in Australia and especially that one day, Australia could exact their revenge on the old enemy.

Over 45 years later, Harry finally got to see the latter, but the former was a more complex beast. He had experienced the highs and lows of two successful and eight unsuccessful tilts at World Cup qualification. It was a similar experience domestically where, as a fan, he had witnessed the rise and decline of the fabulous club football of western Sydney in the 50s and 60s involving clubs such as

Auburn, Leichhardt and Canterbury-Marrickville. And now, the last 20 years had brought the highs and of late, the lows of the National Soccer League.

He was a generation older than the rest of *Bay 23* and not coincidentally the father of three of its members. His loyalty, good nature, opinions delivered at high volume and love of a few beers saw him respected and befriended by all.

Gremlin thought the world of Harry and, in a football sense, saw him as somewhat of a father figure. Similar to a few others in *Bay 23*, Gremlin had moved to Australia some years ago, but his love of football and desire to see Australia do well was far more greatly invested in him than the other Poms with innovative nicknames like Chelsea Rob and Gooner. Only one thing riled the emigrant from the city of Bristol: fans of the hated hometown rival, the Bristol Rovers.

As for Geoff, the northern Sydney suburban born-and-bred character was football personified, both on and off the pitch. He had been playing the game at local club level ever since he could walk and most (including himself) assumed that he would be on the pitch one day in the far distant future and just keel over there and then.

The trio crossed the inner west of Sydney and the talk naturally turned to the afternoon's fixture and the Australian game more generally. Harry was more interested in discussing the latter. "So, who's going to be the new national coach then? I thought young Frank did all right, but the whole bloody squad got no support from Soccer Australia. None! I don't know how these administrators think. Can't they see they are responsible for the running of the game?!"

"As long as it's not Arnold," replied Gremlin from the back seat. He was no fan of the Socceroo star's coaching efforts at Northern Spirit. As he said the word *Arnold,* his Bristolian accent dragged the first syllable as "Arrrr—", making him sound more like a pirate than usual.

They arrived at Belmore Oval. A small contingent of like-minded Spirit fans, the ones they knew well from frequenting the McCartney Terrace back at North Sydney Oval, were congregated close to one of the bars. Beyond that, there couldn't have been more than 2000 Olympic fans in an otherwise oversized venue barely built for football, dominated by a spattering of the seated old faithful with their grandkids running around playing games near the pitch's perimeter fence.

The game dragged on in tedious fashion. Sometimes at North Sydney Oval it was possible to conceive that the NSL was undergoing a new broad-based change, but away, it was business as usual. The guy who sold peanuts across Olympic's various home venues for the past 20 years walked past, spruiking his wares in Greek. The home fans burst into cries of "OL-LYM-PIC!!" at infrequent intervals, the cheering led by their ever-present crazed number one fan, Andrew Hatzioannou.

Harry looked over at the home fans, considered the 1–1 score line and the general state of play, and shook his head. "I don't know where the game is going in this country," he said with melancholy.

Gremlin clapped him on the shoulder. "C'mon, Harry, let's be getting you another beer," he said with a grin.

***

Thirty kilometres away at Edensor Park, David Krilic did the dutiful thing and had sat down to watch Sydney United with his father. It was David's birthday and he had driven with his partner all the way from their newly purchased apartment in Elizabeth Bay for a large extended family lunch for him at the King Tomislav Club. David knew that this was not just about his birthday, but that more importantly he could be shown off to as many wider family and friends as possible. His parents, penniless migrants from Croatia who arrived in the 1950s as part of Australia's post-war migration boom, had established themselves in Australia but more importantly had raised their children with the opportunity for advancement through education. David was the jewel in the crown, having graduated locally at Sydney University in commerce followed by a postgraduate stint at Harvard in Boston.

He was one of the leading lights at a successful Australian-based investment company established by his friend, Spiro, whom he met when overseas. They were both hugely successful when it came to corporate finance and especially investing in flagging enterprises and turning them around.

His aunt made sure everyone knew about it. "He is very wealthy and has been to university twice!" she had remarked more than once.

David knew the club and the associated ground well. He had been well-raised in the traditions and values of Croatian culture and the club was the centrepiece. Much of his early teen years were a great disappointment to his father as when it came to football he had two left feet, but in due course his academic and financial success put to bed any prior paternal scorn.

Krilic the younger knew football well but it had been a long time since he had taken in the local game. Overall, the scene was largely unchanged. The red-and-white chequerboard design was everywhere, the open seating was only partially full and a group of noisy, boisterous young males were behind the goal. After an on-field incident, one lit a flare and threw it onto the pitch.

David glanced at his father through the haze, who shrugged. "Kids," he said gruffly.

The game continued at a pretty decent standard. Krilic recalled that many overseas-based stars and Australian representatives were either Croatian descendant or recruited locally and had come through Sydney United. Almost absent-mindedly, the accounting genius began to turn numbers over in his head.

"Dad," he said shortly. "Many of the club's players have gone on to make millions out of playing in Europe. Surely the club must do pretty well out of that?"

"Nah," his father replied. "All the money goes to agents or somewhere. This place is built on the hard work of those who came before you!"

"Yeah, but overseas, big clubs make a fortune from player transfers. You need to recoup the hard work you all put into the youngsters. And they keep coming—this game is pretty good!" After a beat, he continued "… and why aren't there more people here? This is a national competition and soccer is the biggest sport on the planet. Someone could pull all this together and make a real success of it."

"What do you want to do, buy the fucking place?" retorted his father. David shook his head and smiled, but inside his head the wheels kept turning.

***

David kept thinking all the way home, driving his girlfriend nuts with his silence and infuriating her when he went straight to his study to do some proper research. Poring over his computer, the next few hours were spent reading extensively about professional sports leagues, the fractured and partisan Australian sporting landscape, the history of Australian soccer—not that there was much online— and the game internationally.

Along the way, he started putting indicative numbers onto a newly created spreadsheet. There was a reasonable margin of error, he admitted to himself.

Then he came across it. The Crawford Report into Australian Soccer. A government-commissioned blueprint into how a new national football league might be structured and administered. He immediately spotted some cultural and financial holes in the document, but at least there was a groundswell of individuals across society who could conceive of and propose a better product.

By four a.m. he had completed his dossier and proposal. He shut his laptop and wondered what the boss would make of it.

Chapter 7
Melbourne, Australia,
May 2003

Dinner had finished, and the elderly suited gentlemen leaned back, many lighting cigars. The dimly lit room now became hazy with the rising smoke. Spiro Batsis glanced around the table and literally pinched himself to prevent a smirk. It looked like a scene straight out of *The Godfather.*

But Spiro knew this was no laughing matter. This was the meeting that would make or break the deal; it could undo all the work he and his partner David Krilic had been working on for months, criss-crossing the country, raising capital, setting the course for internal club restructures, and promoting and reinforcing the concept. This meeting was the one that would ultimately determine the fate of the domestic game in Australia.

Finally, Jim Anastasias, the president of South Melbourne, rose to speak. "Gentlemen, dear friends, thank you for joining us today. We acknowledge our friends and brothers from Sydney"—the contingent from Sydney United and Olympic nodded in appreciation—"and also our dear friends from Melbourne Croatia."

At this, Spiro could not repress a slight wince. *This may be harder than we thought.*

Anastasias continued. "As you know, our clubs and the National Soccer League are in dire trouble. These two men, luckily but happily sons of our great peoples, represent a growing group who believe they have the answers for us. For months they have been working with your people, attracting potential investment, inviting us to reform our management. Much has been achieved but everything is yet to be enacted. The time has come for us to decide: are we ready to make the changes being asked of us? Before we discuss that question, let me invite Mr Spiro Batsis of the BKG Investment Group to speak."

Spiro was up. He gave a nervous cough, stood, removed his perfectly tailored Armani suit jacket and opened his leather folder. Here he was, company director, a self-made millionaire many times over, an outstanding product of the great Australian post-war success story, and yet he still felt a moderate anxiety in front of his elders. He glanced across at his business partner and friend David, the accounting genius who had helped propel their careers; his facial expression indicated that he felt the same way. Old world traditions ran deep.

"Mr Anastasias, gentlemen, we thank you for the opportunity to meet today. I know that you are all up to date with the developments and proposals that have been evolving over the last few months, but for clarity we have reproduced the relevant information that you can find in your folders. This evening, I would like to focus on the top line principles and discuss any questions or concerns that you may have."

No mutinies yet.

"Gentlemen, as you know, the National Soccer League is on its last legs. If the league continues as it is, it will inevitably fold within one to two seasons. Your clubs and their members will return to the state leagues. Just as importantly—and I know that you gentlemen have a deep love for soccer and want it to be successful in this country—the game itself here will go backwards."

A pause.

Spiro continued. "The National Federation is, sadly, not well run, and there is little prospect of salvation from Soccer Australia. We can only expect limited help from government. Our politicians have quite rightly questioned why taxpayer money is being directed towards soccer without proper accountability. Their solution was to find a so-called *white knight* to upend the game from top to bottom, but as you know, that hasn't come to pass."

Spiro couldn't tell if the last comment made the old men grimace or smile. They all knew the story. Prime Minister John Howard had asked his sports minister to approach billionaire Frank Lowy, a passionate but self-estranged football fan and one of the founding fathers of the NSL, to consider running Australian soccer. He had turned them down flat. No-one knew exactly why. Perhaps his business empire wouldn't allow enough time, perhaps he wasn't offered the complete control he would have demanded, perhaps even that the offer didn't come from a direct call from Howard himself—but in any event, that door had closed quickly.

"With that," Spiro continued, "it seemed that all hope was lost but, as David and I have continually stressed, the government report by Mr Crawford has unintentionally given us a chance to re-create our own future."

Practically everyone involved in Australian soccer knew about the Crawford Report. There was widespread disquiet as to how government money was being spent in soccer. Pointed questions were being asked in Senates Estimates Hearings as to the accountability of federal funding, doubtless seeded by people close to the sport who wanted change.

In response, government had commissioned prominent businessman David Crawford to conduct a comprehensive review of the game, following extensive research and consultation with multiple stakeholders. With respect to a revitalised national league, the report recommended a new league with clubs that were truly representative of a specific city or geographical region. It also recommended that the league be run independently of the national body, similar to the English Premier League formed in the early 1990s.

"With appropriate structural change, with financial backing, and most importantly with the creation of our own entity that can operate the National Soccer League, we can solve both the government and the Federation's problem for them and do so at a taxpayer cost far less than some alternative new league created out of nothing. Given the weaknesses at Soccer Australia, we can present the new structure and get our new body—the Association of Professional Soccer Clubs— agreed to, with little resistance. And if we get this right, it will be profitable for all of us."

It's time for the kicker.

"But as we have been pushing for the last few months, there are some absolute prerequisites for being a member of the APSC. All member clubs must have their business and financial arrangements structured according to strict principles—what the Americans are now calling appropriate *corporate governance*. In fact, your new investors will not allow anything else. And if we are to be the league aspired to in Crawford's Report, the so-called traditional clubs will need to evolve—not just existing for their historic base, but for the broader community whom they will represent into the future."

Ante Marković, president of Sydney United, leapt to his feet. "Why should we abandon everything we worked hard for? Are we to forget our heritage, our struggles? Are we to turn our backs on our people who formed our clubs? You sound like David Hill, forcing us to change our culture and names. That achieved nothing!"

David Krilic turned to face the irate Ante. "Sir, we mean no disrespect, and nobody is expecting clubs like yours to abandon your heritage. The names Sydney United, Melbourne Knights, Sydney Olympic and South Melbourne are all, yes, to varying degrees recent adaptions but are perfectly appropriate. And we would want your history to continue.

"But we are also in a new world. Look at Spiro and myself. We, like your children, are steeped in our parents' traditions and values and respectful of them. But in our work and our play, we walk in the modern Australian world as well. Our friends and colleagues come from many different backgrounds—some have been in this land for a few years, others for 50,000. Families of many backgrounds have a love of football. Let them into your club and make them welcome at your games. Encourage your young people to bring along all their friends, let them experience what a game day can really be like. They will build a loyalty far beyond the traditional roots of their fathers."

Spiro took over. "In fact, the National Soccer League has the potential to be the only Australian sporting body truly representing the best of this country. Unlike competitor codes, we can set examples in multicultural and Indigenous inclusion, as well as appropriately expanding our women's and youth leagues. We don't have to be the biggest, but we can be the best. That's something I am hoping we could all be proud to be part of."

Marković sat down.

The Knight's president spoke. "That's all very well, but the press will always label us wogs and tear us down at every opportunity."

"I think that will be the case no matter what we do and how we look," replied Spiro. "The newspapers and TV channels, along with their reporters, all benefit from promoting the AFL and rugby league. But new media outlets are emerging. The internet will be an increasingly common way, particularly for young people, to interact and get their news. Our research suggests that within a short number of years, a significant proportion of people under 30 won't even be reading newspapers or watching television as we know it. Our association and its member clubs, with professional help, will be able to connect to our supporters via these new ways and increase their numbers."

Anastasias intervened to redirect the conversation. "So, Spiro, please summarise for us the structure of the proposed revamped league."

"With the agreement of the four clubs represented here, and following discussions with others around the country, the new league will initially consist of ten clubs. Perth Glory, the new Adelaide United and Newcastle are all one-city teams that pick themselves and have acquired the necessary backing. In Brisbane, the Lions are the front runners and just in the last couple of days have shored up their financial backers—"

"Well, they will be very confident after their recent little victory …" interjected Anastasias.

"Indeed," replied Spiro with a smile. "I don't know how much money they got, but it gave them and the code an enormous boost. It shows what can happen when you hold your ground."

They were referring to the AFL's recent blunder when trying to move traditional Victorian club Fitzroy to Queensland. With limited research, the AFL without warning launched a blitzkrieg-style advertising campaign across all media outlets announcing the arrival of the 'Brisbane Lions' to the city. At that point, the existing Brisbane Lions Soccer Club went public, gained an injunction against the illegal use of their name, and promptly sued the AFL for a significant sum. An out-of-court settlement for an undisclosed amount of money resulted in the soccer club defiantly keeping their name. The

AFL briefly retreated with its tail between its legs but re-emerged with a new name for the relocating Fitzroy—'Brisbane Roar'—and successfully spun the whole sorry affair as "a new name for a famous old footy club".

Spiro continued. "That leaves the two big cities of Melbourne and Sydney. Here in Melbourne, the Knights and South. There's also going to be a new franchise playing in central Melbourne, at Olympic Park. What the AFL Soccer Club experiment of Carlton showed is that there is a broader interest in the game, it just wasn't managed very well and frankly, the AFL had a fundamental conflict of interest. You've doubtless heard the rumours and they're true: the new club will be simply called Melbourne City and will play in a red-and-white-striped strip.

"In Sydney, we have Northern Spirit, Olympic and Sydney United. Collectively, those six clubs from the two large cities have their own distinct geographical territory, just as Crawford had suggested."

Spiro turned to the contingent from Sydney Olympic. "How are your relocation plans proceeding?" The question was a little rhetoric as he was well across the club's intention to fill the vacancy left by the departure of the St George club from the NSL some years earlier. "Very well, thank you. As you know, with the generous help of Mr Politis, we will soon be based at St George Stadium and we have plans to transform the ground into a fabulous all-seated venue."

Changing the subject, Marković raised the elephant in the room. "What about those existing NSL clubs that haven't made the cut?"

"Quite frankly, they either haven't been able to raise their side of the capital required or haven't implemented sufficient change to their corporate structures. If their corporate governance gets up to scratch, they can be included in due course. Some have seemed very unwilling, but I suspect they may change their tune over the next couple of seasons. The ultimate goal is to have a 16-team league, so there is still time and space—along with the possibility of other regions like Wollongong, Canberra and Tasmania—to join."

Now the questions came more quickly.

"Do you envisage promotion and relegation?"

"Not for some years. We need stability and financial security before we could even consider that path."

"I still can't see how this will pay for itself …"

"It will be a combination of financial backing, corporate sponsorship including from Virgin Blue to cover air transport, government assistance and most importantly, television broadcast revenue. We are in final negotiations with Foxtel and SBS for a shared broadcast model. We would get more money from an exclusive Foxtel deal, but we believe it's vital to have soccer on free-to-air television."

"Who's talking to government? Can we trust them?"

"Our lobbyists are the best in the business. As I said, what we're after is modest. Medium term, we have plans for infrastructure sports grants to improve those stadia the clubs own and run. Some are in important swinging Federal seats …" Spiro said with a wink.

"Won't that cost a fortune?"

"Not as much as you think. It's feasible to create a 10-to-20,000-seat boutique stadium without too much money or effort. And remember, some clubs are playing out of established or shared facilities—such as Perth, Adelaide and Spirit who are moving to Brookvale in a year's time. An added advantage is that most games will be played on turf that is purpose-built and maintained for proper football."

Anastasias looked around the room. "Well?" he proffered.

Marković again stood up and raised his glass of raki. "Here's to the new APSC and the NSL!!!" The toast was joined in by all.

Spiro looked over at David and grinned. It had been luck, but equally a stroke of genius that the two main movers and shakers hailed from Greek and Croatian backgrounds respectively.

There was an exclusive high-end bar five minutes away in a taxi. Once they took their leave from their elders and their toasts, the two corporate success stories would celebrate long and hard with multiple rounds of their preferred single malt Scotch.

Chapter 8
Sydney, Australia,
July 2003

David Krilic breathed a sigh of relief as the press conference concluded. He had watched the entire circus from the sidelines and was thoroughly glad that he was not one of those in the hot seat, staring into bright lights and under an oversized banner with a new National Soccer League logo. The questions had been coming thick and fast for the last hour or so.

They had all expected this, of course. After all, they were announcing the overhaul of a moribund 25-year-old national sporting competition and were loudly proclaiming a new dawn. Several of the press had been reporting on football for years and their scepticism was understandable.

David was impressed at the way Tony Townsend, the new head of operations at the Association of Professional Soccer Clubs, along with Remo Nogarotto representing club owners had handled the melee. Spiro was his usual financial hard-headed self and had faced far worse at annual general meetings populated by hostile shareholders.

Townsend had done well outlining the basic premise of the new controlling entity and the terms of the relationship between themselves and Soccer Australia. He had correctly drawn parallels with the English Premier League and the Football Association in England and reminded everyone that the model was effectively that which was recommended in the Crawford Report.

The new arrangement meant that the coalition of APSC clubs, henceforth to be part of the revamped NSL, had collectively reached a binding agreement with Soccer Australia to run as an independent entity. Under the terms of the franchise, the NSL would operate under a framework agreed to by both parties, but ultimately the league was answerable to Soccer Australia with respect to several fundamental aspects. Soccer Australia would receive an agreed revenue annually from the league but in other respects, the new NSL would be responsible for its own marketing, television rights negotiations and organisational running costs. Furthermore, the NSL had committed to running a women's league as well as a national youth league to ensure a continued pathway for professional player development into the future.

The principles were straightforward and, as Townsend had pointed out, completely consistent with the federal government's intentions—after all, government remained a stakeholder.

However, the journalists were more interested in the tin tacks and had been relentless in trying to prise specific details as to how the whole thing would work and most importantly, where the money was coming from.

Despite his financial projections, David had his own doubts about this aspect himself.

Then there was the issue that the strategy was built around competing at traditional suburban football grounds—most notably in Sydney and Melbourne—and shunning larger, more modern shared-use facilities.

Michael Lynch from *The Age* was not unsurprisingly interested in the specific dynamics of this and how the new NSL would function in Melbourne.

"I accept that you have the basics of stadia in Melbourne but there is much work to be done. Lakeside needs attention and at Somers Street, you have a grassed area surrounding a football pitch with only one stand on one side. A similar situation exists in Sydney in St George Stadium, where I see Olympic are moving to. How are you possibly going to get the resources to establish these grounds as acceptable standard football stadia for fans to attend in comfort? And then you have the new club Melbourne City, a team to be started from scratch with no confirmed stadium to play in?"

"Let me speak to the issue of Melbourne City first," replied Townsend. "As you know, discussions are well advanced with the Victorian Government for a new Olympic Park, a rectangular ground that will be the home of both the new Melbourne City soccer club and the Melbourne Storm rugby league club. The government has given us a firm commitment that the stadium will be completed within the next few years. In the interim Melbourne City have stated they would likely play at the existing Olympic Park. I can assure you the Victorian Government recognises that Olympic Park is the last remaining asset in their impressive sporting precinct that requires a major overhaul. There *will* be a Melbourne rectangular stadium and there will be a successful Melbourne City club that will be calling the stadium home."

Townsend continued. "With respect to Lakeside, South Melbourne already have an impressive facility there, but we do have plans to revitalise the grandstands and improve seating at both ends of the ground. And as far as Knights Stadium goes, like St George Stadium in Sydney we have the vision to create boutique football grounds that will be a tremendous game day experience for both players and fans."

Lynch was persistent. "But where do you possibly think you will get sufficient funds to turn stadia like Somers Street into an acceptable 15-to-20,000-capacity venue?"

"Our financial backers, the BKG Investment Group, have every intention of underwriting, through loans, towards the refurbishment of these grounds," Townsend replied as he turned to acknowledge Spiro Batsis sitting next to him. "There is new television revenue. We also have the expectation of assistance in the form of government grants and of course contributions from each local club. We call this overarching strategy the National Stadium Project."

Much of the press gallery took this part with a grain of salt, others were distinctly nonplussed, and the remainder frankly incredulous.

Mike Cockerill from *The Sydney Morning Herald* was willing at least to cut them some slack with respect to stadium development.

"Tony, this is an ambitious move for the football community in this country and an exciting proposal. I'm more interested about the geography and dynamics in Sydney. Several large NSL clubs, most notably Marconi, are not part of the new arrangement. You also have a large gap in territory, containing potentially hundreds of thousands of football fans between Sydney United at Edensor Park and Olympic playing out of St George Stadium. How does this fit with the Crawford Report, and do you propose to cater for their football needs at a national competition level, moving forward?"

"The competition for next season is just the beginning," Townsend replied. "We have every intention of expanding the league in due course. As we have stated, there were strict conditions of entry and membership of the APSC. That was essential to ensure the NSL's organisational and financial survival. Applications for entry remain open, including for season two and beyond. I suspect you will find that existing and even new clubs will emerge that can meet the relevant hurdles, hopefully not just in, but beyond Sydney and Melbourne."

Craig Foster from SBS changed the direction of the conversation. "Look, it's great that your aim is to maintain the history of the game and in particular the presence of the post-war clubs and their communities. But how do you propose to ensure a much wider representation in attendance, and, frankly, interest from the general Australian public?"

Nogarotto replied, "The clubs will be operating under a strict charter and terms of agreement. There is no plan to reign in aspects of their heritage but there is a strong obligation upon them to expand their audience and fan base to the general population, in particular to the district in which they are operating. It is a condition of the ongoing membership of the APSC and the NSL that these principles are strictly adhered to, along with financial performance as well as fundamental operational and corporate governance."

He added, "Furthermore, clubs like Northern Spirit, Newcastle, Adelaide and Perth demonstrate that football already has a stronghold in the broader Australian community."

"And in turn, I think many of the so-called migrant communities would like to see the NSL truly represent multicultural Australia in all its respects," returned Foster.

The notebooks and the cameras had enough content for their various editors' deadlines to be met and the press conference wound up. As they filed out of the room, Michael Lynch caught long-time football reporter Ray Gatt's vision and raised his eyebrows. "They'll be broke in two years," said Ray.

Chapter 9

Sydney, Australia,

April 2004

Spiro Batsis had just settled into his plush chair behind his imposing desk. His office at BKG's headquarters had commanding views of Sydney Harbour from a 25-storey vantage point. It was a bright, warm, sunny day outside, with yachts and their crews taking advantage of the late summer conditions on the shimmering blue water. He took his eyes away from the vista but before he could get to his board papers, his executive assistant politely knocked on the door.

"Yes, Jane?"

"Sorry to trouble you so early, sir, but I've had a rather strange call from someone in Russia who would like to discuss stadium construction with you."

Spiro had tried repeatedly to get Jane to use his first name, but his curiosity over the call caused him to overlook it this time.

"Russia?" he asked with genuine surprise.

"Yes, Nakhodka." She had a reply before Batsis could get the obvious question in. "I looked it up. It's close to Vladivostok, on Russia's Pacific seaboard."

About our time zone, Spiro thought absently before he returned to the conversation. "Are you sure this isn't some kind of prank?"

"I don't think so. The gentleman, Slava Meyn his name is, has sent through a lot of documentation about himself and his businesses. If the reports are to be believed, he's very wealthy. He's also a big football fan and states that he has a keen interest in Australia and New Zealand."

Ten to one this is some kind of Russian mafia scam, Spiro mused. "Well, forward me the documents and let me look through them. If I'm comfortable, we can set up a call."

***

Spiro concluded the phone call, his mind racing and turning over possibilities. Throughout the two-hour conversation, his mood had shifted from scepticism to piqued interest through to excitement at what was being proposed.

BKG's research had confirmed Meyn's credentials: he was everything his documentation had suggested and more.

A self-made millionaire many times over, Meyn was one of those people who could spot business opportunities, thought laterally, and importantly could establish and execute the most complex projects with efficiency and cost effectiveness. His hometown of Nakhodka had a population of less than 200,000 people, but it didn't stop Meyn from starting a business importing toys, furniture and construction materials from China in the early 1990s.

From there his company upscaled significantly in the area of building materials and in particular modular housing construction. From a retail outlet business in Nakhodka, he quickly developed joint ventures with several overseas companies.

Having become an expert in modular construction, overseas acquisition of raw materials and import/export in general, Meyn had lately turned his attention to applying these concepts to football stadia.

In short, Meyn could foresee the future of football across the planet and how it should be staged. Outside of the big leagues, stadia needed to be compact, comfortable and affordable. With the progressive growth of pay television, crowds of the future would reduce in size, but game day experience would remain the most important component in maintaining viable attendances. That meant rectangular stadia for the rectangular game, closeness to the action, and compactness, significantly accelerating the atmosphere. For marquee games, there was a risk of sell-out, but this merely added to the value of attendance and in particular season ticket sales. Above all, it didn't have to be plush—corporate boxes, suites and restaurants, the obsessions of large stadia, were all unnecessary and simply added cost that couldn't be recouped. Last but by no means least, leagues like the NSL should at all costs confine itself to soccer-only grounds to ensure the pitch standard for the vast majority of the games.

All of that made perfect sense, but it was how this was being achieved that was the real music to Spiro's ears.

Several grounds around the world had already begun using modular construction techniques—entire stadium stands could be manufactured in China, with sections shipped to the city in question and assembled on site, saving perhaps millions of dollars on traditional construction costs. A project could be started and completed quickly around the ground, with some components, such as the behind goal areas and roofing, added later.

Meyn was already planning to apply many of these ideas at FC Okean Nakhodka, of which the football-mad Russian was now president. But he didn't plan on sitting tight, either in business or in geography.

Incredibly, Slava Meyn had plans to relocate his family to New Zealand, where he wanted to undertake an entire football project there—stadium, training pitches, academy, the whole caboodle—but he would need to crown the project with a National Soccer League Club that would be the first in an expanded Trans-Tasman—maybe even an Oceania-wide—league.

Compared with the rejected Auckland Kings, Meyn's vision, football smarts and wealth would blow the former Kiwi bid out of the park and it would be impossible not to embrace it.

In return, Meyn would be more than happy to share his contacts and nous with the national league more generally, particularly in achieving a common standard when it came to facilities and pitch quality. It was an offer too good to refuse.

Spiro Batsis leaned back in his chair and stared out over the harbour with a broad smile. The missing link that would ensure the success of the National Stadium Project had just found him.

Chapter 10

Sydney, Australia,

July 2005

Stefan Kamasz arrived early at Soccer Australia headquarters, ready for the lengthy meeting ahead of the executive group. He pushed through the glass doors and past the Federation's two most prized possessions, proudly displayed in the foyer and gleaming within their respective Perspex cabinets.

The first, the Oceania Nations Cup, was an enduring near-permanent fixture that could be traced back to 1980. No matter that Australia had to do nothing to keep the trophy until the tournament was resurrected in 1996. But a commitment to the event, inspired by World Cup qualification and a leaning on, politically and monetarily, by FIFA meant that Australia's concerted efforts had led to a continuous holding on to the title and the silverware for over two decades.

Soccer Australia officials often quipped that the trophy should be bolted down, America's Cup style, with the matching ceremonial spanner hidden in the chairman's arse. Such was the routine expectation that the Champions of Oceania would be unchanging, tournament after tournament.

However, it was the second trophy, the under 17 Men's World Cup, that commanded more respect amongst the faithful.

Won in 1999, it was the only world trophy ever won by an Oceania side, made all the sweeter as it was won on rival Kiwi home soil to boot. Having progressed through a tough group that consisted of both Germany and Brazil, the young Australians found themselves, on paper at least, on a relatively straightforward passage through to the final. There they met Ghana who had squeezed their way past Brazil in their semi-final on penalties.

The youngsters were clearly anxious and tightened up significantly in one of the nation's most important ever football matches. Ghana had the better of the match but failed to put the game away, then on 79 minutes Scott McDonald tapped home from inside the six-yard box after an untidy defensive effort from the Africans. A nervy backs-to-the-wall final 15 minutes ensued when at last, the referee blew full time and wild celebrations began.

Amongst the general public, the game had drawn far less interest, somewhat understandably, than the senior side's efforts in *France '98*, but for the purists it was an incredibly important outcome and vindicated Australia's long investment and love affair with men's youth tournaments. Given just two senior qualifications since Australia's World Cup quest began in 1965, from the early 1980s the local fascination with world youth cups began in earnest, firstly on home soil in 1981 and poignantly with a defeat of Argentina in Sydney, in the nation's first outing in that series. From there, it was a rollicking ride every two years, including a further hosting in the early 1990s with the under-20 side earning a credible fourth place. Now there was also an under-17 tournament to embrace and of course, some years ago, the Olympics had essentially become an under-23 event.

Running parallel to all of this was the progressive development of international women's events.

Collectively, there was a lot to support and celebrate about, in both the women and men's international teams at all levels. In the women's game there was clear cut-through from Sunday park football to the national team and a direct qualification pathway to all world football tournaments. For the men, continued success suggested that although the *golden generation* was already at its peak, it was possible that the pipeline of talented youngsters might continue. Soccer Australia had to accept, however, that as in past days truly talented individuals might get snapped up by overseas clubs very early and additionally that professional youth development was now actually in the hands of the APSC. Thankfully, so far, the newly privatised and independent structure had stuck by their commitment to a national youth league, both in design (a legal requirement of course) and in philosophy.

***

The meeting commenced. Kamasz glanced around the board table. As newly appointed CEO of Soccer Australia—and having departed from this role within the NSL following the league's unbundling—he was in a unique position. Amongst his many duties, he was responsible for maintaining good relations with the APSC and thus far everyone remained on fairly decent terms. It helped that the APSC had, to date, paid their licence fees in full and on time.

Today, however, the main topic of discussion was their recent deliberations with FIFA and the fact they had achieved what they had collectively agreed was a highly satisfactory outcome. For the 2006 and 2010 editions of the men's World Cup, Oceania, with no small input and leadership from Soccer Australia, had successfully negotiated that the confederation's inter-continental playoff would take place against the fifth best Asian team. The dangers of meeting another South American team had been avoided for at least eight years.

It hadn't been easy; in fact, it had been diabolically difficult and a near-run thing. The cause hadn't been helped by David Hill's grandstanding over joining the Asian Football Confederation only a couple of years earlier, leading to a resounding and embarrassing put-down by FIFA. For decades, Australia's on again and off again quest to move from Oceania to the AFC had been batted away and was now effectively dead and buried.

And then there was Charlie Dempsey.

Dempsey, the dour Scot, had emigrated to New Zealand in 1952 and had worked his way through football administration in his adopted country to head the Oceania Football Confederation from the early 1980s onwards. Probably because of Australia's prior disdain of Oceania, possibly because he just didn't like the bigger brother across the ditch, he was a thorn in Soccer Australia's side at every turn. When Australia won the continental championship in Canberra in the 1990s, he refused to even acknowledge Australia as the winners as he reluctantly handed over the trophy. In *France '98* he was nowhere to be seen, certainly not backing Oceania's first representative for 16 years.

None of that would have mattered, certainly at FIFA level, except for his actions in 1999 when, as a member of FIFA executive, the pressure of a crucial vote to determine where the 2006 World Cup be held became too much and he had absented himself. That decision led to the tournament being awarded to Germany rather than the FIFA hierarchy's favoured South Africa.

With Oceania variously offside with Africa and Asia and with South America sniffing for an 'easy' further qualification place, there was a lot of spade work to do. Thankfully, Hill had departed after the

2002 qualification failure and Dempsey's beacon from Auckland was progressively fading. For two years no one had even been sure what residual role he had in the confederation, but for at least a year he seemed to have finally been sidelined.

There had been some smart lobbying but in the end, the sheer weight and size of the AFC, with their own self-interest of meeting Oceania in the playoffs rather than South America, won the day. Simple geography also played a role—Asia and Oceania, and North/ Central and South America were more common-sense matchups, but as always with FIFA, no decision could ever be guaranteed on the basis of common sense.

So, whilst as usual Oceania was not deemed to be worthy of a direct qualification position, despite now being a full-blown confederation in its own right and the World Cup finals now a 32-team affair, at least there was a palatable and slightly more predictable path to the world's greatest event. For the time being, anyway.

The executive agreed to develop a strategy as to how they could wrest, or at least gain steerage over, the administration of Oceania. It was decided to have something for the board within the next 12 months.

The meeting wound up after largely routine housekeeping. In particular, the final corporate revamping of the Federation, forced upon it by government and the departure of the NSL from its immediate watch, was implemented. A better corporate structure and accountability were now in place, with custodianship of the multiple national teams as well as the enormous and diverse grassroots game. All of this was to be paid for by the NSL licence fee, some national team TV money, a modest stipend from government and registration fees. If only there weren't layers of state federations and officialdom, all demanding their share.

***

Four months later, Kamasz sat in the official box for the second leg of the AFC/OFC playoff between Bahrain and Australia at Homebush Stadium.

The qualification pathway had followed its usual progress through the early phases. There were heavy defeats handed to New Caledonia and Tonga, followed up with a couple of bruising home-and-away encounters with Fiji. Even at this early juncture, Soccer Australia had begun a diplomatic but firm policy of demanding the release of Socceroos for international duty, with variable success. Club managers, especially in England, were openly hostile to the principle of their players, who were paid by their owners, flying halfway around the world for what they considered to be essentially meaningless fixtures. A FIFA mandate that any player selected for national duty could not play for his club during a specified time had little teeth if the player suddenly developed an 'injury' leading into the relevant fixture. The risk of being on the wrong side of a semi-professional tackle on a cow paddock, combined with jetlag upon return, weighed heavily on the minds of European masters.

Diplomacy notwithstanding, Australia had begun to rely upon the nation's world class resources in sports science to help overcome many of the challenges, but the time was approaching when formal international breaks would be needed. National representation for both continental tournaments and World Cup qualifiers was an issue right across the planet, not only for Oceania.

A bidding war of sorts had broken out between Melbourne and Sydney for the remaining qualification fixtures. For Soccer Australia, Homebush's Olympic Stadium was the preferred venue for the eventual inter-continental playoff, which meant appeasing the Melburnians with the New Zealand home fixture, the Kiwis having equally strolled through their half of the Pacific matches. There were concerns that the cavernous MCG would lead to a hollow atmosphere if there were a poor attendance, but the Federation needn't have worried. Over 50,000 fans turned up for the Trans-Tasman classic, with the Socceroos carrying the advantage of an away goal following a 1–1 draw in Auckland. Many in the crowd were new fans of the respective three Victorian NSL teams, combined with long-standing soccer tragics and of course Melbourne's infamous record of spectacular attendance at sporting events of any persuasion.

The game itself was a near-run thing. Unlike a year previously, when the All Whites gave a poor account of themselves at the Oceania Nations Cup, this latest Kiwi outfit put in a more determined shift. They opened the scoring early with a well-headed goal from Vaughan Coveny off an outswinging corner kick. The Australians had trouble working the ball in attack, with the New Zealand defence well-disciplined and breaking down play in the home team's final third at almost every opportunity.

In the 43rd minute, however, John Aloisi received the ball 20 metres out and charged at the Kiwi goal. A clumsy defensive effort in the box on the Australian striker resulted in the referee immediately pointing to the spot.

Moore stepped up and calmly slammed the ball into the bottom left-hand corner to bring the tie level.

In the second half, the Australians moved up a gear and the New Zealand defence increasingly began to falter. On 68 minutes, Kewell scored and from there the Kiwis never recovered, ensuring the Socceroos got to appear in the hard-fought-for playoff against Asian opponents just as they had done eight years earlier.

The Asian qualifiers were drawing to a close but, given the two third-placed teams from the AFC's respective final groups were West Asian, Soccer Australia knew they would have some climatic and geographical challenges. A solid 3–1 victory by the Bahrainis at home and a goalless draw away in the Omani capital Muscat determined the Socceroos' opponents. Shortly after, a fortunate decision by FIFA to play the first leg in the Arabian Gulf meant the Federation could finalise their logistics.

For the final home-and-away tie, the cards were falling nicely for Australia. The nation's European stars arrived at the Gulf directly from their respective clubs, well ahead of game time and injury free. It was early November with the temperature bearable and an evening kick-off time had been scheduled with an experienced European referee. Everything was set and the Socceroos didn't disappoint, holding a 2–0 lead until just before full time when a fluky counter from the locals upset the television-tuned parties down under.

The tie was very much alive as Kamasz looked around from his corporate box on Level 3 at Stadium Australia. The match had officially sold out two days prior and all he could see was wall to wall green and gold, aside from a tiny pocket of Bahraini support in one corner.

More importantly, it was a cool evening and word from the dugout was that the visitors were tired. In contrast, the Australians were ready to go, the Federation having learned their lesson from four years ago with respect to flights, ticketing, and even providing some inflight medical and physio assistance.

It all showed on the pitch, although in truth the punters would have loved a few more goals. Instead, a mostly subdued and increasingly nervous crowd roared with a collective outpouring of excitement and relief on 55 minutes when Skoko sent the ball wide to Goodes, who turned inside his defender and drilled a low ball into the left-hand corner of the net, from the opposite outer corner of the penalty box. From there the mood on the pitch and in the stands moved to a crescendo in the last ten minutes, with pandemonium as the full-time whistle sounded.

It had been a tactical masterstroke to appoint Bora Milutinović to coach the Socceroos. Recruited after his successful management of different nations at the previous five World Cups, his latest side were now on their way to Germany. It would be Australia's third World Cup appearance and the survivors from the 2002 campaign would get their chance, along with their rookie teammates, to emulate the exploits of 1998.

Chapter 11

Sydney, Australia,

February 2007

Two thousand dollars! Shit.

Johnny Warren sat at his desk at Soccer Australia and examined the bar bill from the Intercontinental Hotel. The annual Former Socceroos Dinner had always run on a tight budget and there was certainly no room in it for unexpected extra costs. Every year there was a battle with Soccer Australia administrators over holding it and every year Johnny felt he had to go cap in hand to them, despite the fact that he was a board member and *despite* the fact that the event kept former internationals in touch, something he believed quite strongly in. Past Australian teams, whether they had qualified for a World Cup or not, needed to be respected and connected to the present. Even more so after another successful World Cup campaign the year before, where the Socceroos reached the round of 16, only to be snuffed out by a wily and fast-improving Spanish side.

He knew the details—after all, he was there. The prepaid bar tab was fully expensed and duly closed. However, during some extended and (mostly) good-natured banter as to the relevant strengths of different squads, several rounds of Scotch, 'cleansing ales' and other drinks had been ordered and consumed. Wilson insisted in no uncertain terms that the Federation be sent the bill.

Despite the rowdiness, the night had concluded on good terms but there were times when Johnny Warren regretted that he and Noddy Alston had talked Peter Wilson out of his self-imposed isolation.

No matter how you counted 'A' and 'B' internationals—and that was still being debated by the *pro bono* History and Legacy Team—Peter Wilson was by far the most capped Australian captain in the game's history.

Born and raised into football in northeast England, Wilson emigrated to the south coast of New South Wales in 1969. He began his Australian career with South Coast United and was drafted into the Socceroo setup shortly afterwards. He first captained his adopted country in 1971 and in due course played every minute of every qualifier for the 1974 World Cup. From there, he led the side for the three Australian games at the West German edition of the world's greatest tournament.

His international record was paralleled by his stellar club and NSL career. Aside from South Coast united and Marconi, when the NSL formed in 1977 he led Western Suburbs admirably and later played for APIA.

The exact reasons were uncertain, but on retirement he retreated from the game and the public gaze to the quiet and familiar surrounds of Kembla Grange. Doubtless there was major disgruntlement with the game's administrators. But apart from a close inner circle of former teammates, any attempt to engage with Wilson, especially from the press, was met with stiff resistance. He seemed to have a greater interest in motorcycles than Australian football.

After he missed the motorcade before the Iran game in '97, several of the 1974 squad pleaded that something be done to mend ties with

Wilson. Adrian Alston was the best teammate contact and Warren was a board member of SA with special responsibility for former players, history and multicultural engagement. John was no true friend of Wilson's given the captaincy issue back in the early '70s, but in 2005 put aside his differences and agreed that he and Alston should do their best.

They would still have failed if it wasn't for football historian and Wilson's closest contact Andre Kruger coming to the rescue.

Andre, the mercurial German whose love of Australia from early childhood had led him on the most unexpected of life journeys. Born in 1960 in Hanover, from early childhood Andre developed a love of things Australian and everything about that faraway country. With his nation's hosting of the World Cup in 1974 drawing closer, as a young teenager he determined that Australia was his team, his mother creating a Socceroos jersey for him that he could wear when he and the local kids were playing out their street versions of the tournament.

Following *WM '74*, he continued his fascination with Australian football and the 1974 Socceroos in particular. As a young adult he joined a merchant ship to see the world and got his first taste of Australia in the early 1980s. On shore leave in Sydney, he travelled to outer suburban Dural to watch Wilson play. For Andre, Wilson was the greatest of Socceroos and unrivalled before or since.

Otherwise, in the pre-internet era, Andre's time was spent in Germany collecting memorabilia, photos, videos, press clippings, *anything* to do with the Socceroos. He began to establish friendships with Australian football fans and players alike and refashioned himself as something of an aficionado on Australian soccer history and a major collector of memorabilia.

He had begun to visit Australia in the early 2000s and had personally witnessed the final 2001 and 2005 home qualifiers. But as his view of Europe and the country of his birth began to sour, he decided, hard as it was, that it was time to permanently move to the country in his heart.

They had been mail contacts for years, and following his emigration from Germany in 2004 and settling with his wife Sabine in the Wollongong region, Andre had connected with and become very dependent on Peter Wilson in adjusting to Australian life. The pair met regularly, including a number of motorcycle rides taken together through the Southern Highlands. Andre seemed to have given Wilson a new lease on life, who reluctantly agreed to a story on SBS Television.

The media piece was a clunky affair—in fact, it was mostly stock game footage and only a few words from Wilson, given his aversion to being in the spotlight—but it seemed to spark something in him. It gave him licence to comment on any and everything that he felt was wrong with Australian soccer. It was great television, with Andy Paschalidis from SBS heading to Wollongong every two weeks to do a one-on-one with Wilson at the local pub. No-one was spared any barbs, with Soccer Australia now finding themselves in a bind: on the one hand, a great historic riff had been mended with the cultural importance of having the '74 captain back in the tent, but on the other hand, 'Big Willie', as he was nicknamed, had no hesitation in pissing in it.

In any event, Wilson began regularly attending international games whenever they were in Sydney and, without fail, both the TV coverage and the big stadium screens took great delight in showing his entry into the ground and taking his seat, complete with his bikie leathers and his impressive beard, ZZ Top style.

And of course, he had begun participating in Socceroos functions.

Warren put down the bill. *The Federation will just have to pay it*, he concluded. After all, he had bigger things on his plate. The executive and the board, along with the APSC and the Professional Players' Association, were midway through a major overhaul of the players' contract and transfer system.

As if that wasn't enough, he was also part of a working group looking into junior football development and how best to foster increasing participation along with the progression of playing standards and style in the game. Now opened, this was a massive can of worms.

Warren wanted any actions arising from the working group's review extended to junior clubs and especially 'Academies', privately run entities usually consisting of a prior player or coach with connections to an overseas club or talent agents. There was growing concern that these outfits were running their own development style and convincing parents to part with significant sums of money, having advised Mum and Dad that little Johnny or little Jill was surely the next big thing, if only they were given the right pathway. Bringing those groups into a national framework would be tough.

Then there was the task of ensuring the national youth league kept in step with the overarching strategic directions of Soccer Australia with respect to player development as well as fostering appropriate career pathways, as young players progressed from grassroots clubs.

Finally, there was the travesty of the gradual demise of football's stake in the Australian Institute of Sport and the Federation's eleventh-hour lobbying with government to maintain the game's presence, or indeed return it to the glory days when it regularly produced Socceroos of high calibre.

Somehow, these elements all needed to be adapted and drawn together with common purpose and maybe, but controversially, with an agreed strategic playing style. Personally, Warren wanted a common overarching pattern of play yet to still keep a focus on individualism. He was biased, he admitted to himself, but he longed to develop a national program of South American-style football without losing the traditional rugged and direct Australian national team approach.

Whether that was possible or desired was another question altogether.

There was so much to do, and he was tired and out of breath, despite being seated. He had an enormous rasping coughing fit and noticed, for the first time, blood in the used tissue. *Shit*, he thought.

***

Despite extensive treatment including aggressive chemotherapy, Johnny Warren died of lung cancer in February 2008. His one regret was that he was a heavy smoker and that he didn't give it up sooner, belatedly becoming a national figure for the anti-smoking cause. But his tireless work for the Federation had contributed to promoting, improving and developing the game at all levels. Further, he lived to see the Socceroos return to the world stage in 1998 in style, after a quarter of a century's absence. And after the victory over the Netherlands in Toulouse, on reports that back in Australia hundreds of thousands of people had celebrated in the early hours of the morning on the streets of Sydney, Melbourne and across the country, he was asked for comment.

He famously responded with, "I told you so."

Chapter 12
Sydney, Australia,
May 2008

Spiro Batsis took his morning coffee and his home-delivered copy of *The Sydney Morning Herald*'s Saturday edition out onto the balcony of his Mosman home. It was early on a sunny morning; birdsong rang from the trees below and in the distance Mosman Bay was glasslike. Shortly, he would need to get his kids off to Saturday morning soccer, so Spiro went straight to the sports section to read the review he knew was included. Pleasingly, the extended article by Michael Cockerill was just the second page into the sport section and sat right next to the match report from the previous evening's Sydney derby between Northern Spirit and Olympic.

NSL Report Card

Five years on from the near collapse and restructure of the NSL, SMH's football journalist Michael Cockerill assesses how Australia's longest-running national sporting competition is faring.

In 2003, the National Soccer League was bottom of the class and threatened with expulsion from the Australian sporting school. Crowds were at an all-time low with the organisational and financial situation in a perilous state. But thanks to a better and united business model, appropriate governance and the creation of an independent body to manage the league, the NSL's grades have improved. Let's look at a number of areas and see what has been achieved and what still needs to be done.

Organisational structure 8/10

The Crawford Report in 2003 proposed a newly created regional-based competition, with no involvement of the traditional 'ethnic' clubs. Furthermore, the report recommended that a new league should be run as an independent structure under licence to Soccer Australia— effectively the model under which the English Premier League is run. Rightly or wrongly, no 'white knight' or entity came forward to design and build a new league—but financiers and backers came to the aid of the NSL to implement the proposed independent structure within the existing league, leading to the creation of the Association of Professional Soccer Clubs (APSC) which continues to successfully run the NSL five years later. Membership came at a price and with signing on to significant club reform, particularly with respect to sound business principles and corporate governance. Broad regional inclusiveness was demanded with a view to widening the makeup of their members and attendees at games. More of that later.

Stadia 6/10

Still a work in progress. While some of the clubs lease multipurpose venues, many, including the older clubs, have embarked on a program to utilise their existing ground ownership and upgrade seating and stands. The APSC call this the 'National Stadium Project'. Money has been tight particularly as, more often than not, government funds have been directed towards larger expensive AFL venues, undoubtedly for political purposes. However, the league has secured some ongoing government assistance for the project, along with borrowings and utilising shared profits from television revenue. They have, rather ingeniously, used modular construction techniques with offshore construction of stadium components that are shipped to Australia with local assembly. This has reduced the cost of creating stadia significantly. The results are 10,000–20,000 person capacity venues, perfect for local football. The basic seating structures are largely in place; however, better amenities under the seating shells and roofing have barely been embarked upon. But they will come.

Crowds 7/10

NSL administration has demanded that the older, culturally specific clubs open up and expand their community base and membership. Clubs were able to respect and preserve their history, but they were expected to provide a game day experience for everyone, irrespective of their background. In fact, it is a contractual part of the deal. Families in particular were to be encouraged.

Crowd attendance and the experience on the day has been particularly bolstered by organised fan groups, particularly behind goal ends. Across the world such support is a potential for trouble. However, NSL fans have instead generally created a colourful, boisterous atmosphere with shared banners and songs. They are well organised, particularly younger fans who are now using platforms like Facebook to connect, organise themselves and to get their football news, rather than by the traditional printed press. The seemingly ingrained indifference of newspapers to football in this country does not hold them back.

Going to the football is now a cool pastime. The result? From a low point of attendances around the 1,000-mark, average attendances are around 7,500 with derbies enjoying crowds in the 10,000 to 20,000 range.

Playing standards 5/10

The national league, indeed, the entire Australian football landscape, continues to produce quality players. However, the most talented footballers either leave our shores early or are transferred in an inconsistent fashion to overseas clubs, often with little reward for the investment in developing them. A diverse and at times self-interested collection of predominantly private 'football academies' across the country doesn't help. A more equitable national standard of player transfers, including international transfers, is coming next year, but reform is needed from top to bottom.

Irrespective of this, the increasing exposure of overseas football leagues on cable television shows a significant divide between standards, in particularly Europe and here. Nonetheless, full-time professionalism, a national youth league with progression to the senior leagues, high quality football-only pitches at most of the venues and 'active' crowd support all help to maintain a product of good enough quality.

Geographical coverage 7/10

True national coverage—a team in each major region of significant size— is almost there. The original 10 APSC members quickly incorporated Marconi and Canberra United by the third season.

Some obvious gaps and one anomaly remain. When Marconi joined— reportedly after initially dragging their heels, followed by a rapid recognition as to how important their NSL membership was to all concerned—Sydney was left with two southwestern teams only a couple of kilometres apart, with an enormous gap between them and Olympic and Northern Spirit on the southern and northern sides of the harbour respectively. The long-mooted inclusion of the start-up club Sydney Rovers based at Parramatta is well overdue. As is the entry of the Brisbane Strikers to create the much-loved derby experience up north, that Sydney and Melbourne fans enjoy on a recurring basis.

With two positions available to complete the APSC's original strategic plan of 16 clubs, some jostling remains. The Victorian football community quite rightly argue that the league is already Sydney-centric and getting worse. There is also a strong case for a Tasmanian team and rumours abound of a joint franchise playing out of Launceston, Hobart and Geelong. And waiting in the wings is the impressively resourced Christchurch United, owned by the cashed-up Russian-turned-Kiwi, Slava Meyn, who is progressively turning New Zealand football on its head. It's a poorly kept secret that Meyn provided assistance and many of the contacts to the APSC with their Stadium Project. That assistance will be rewarded, and quite frankly the NSL will grow and succeed at a faster rate with Meyn's team on board, as it emulates the NRL in including a team from the Shaky Isles.

Television coverage 6/10

The league's revitalised television deal included a renewed contract for five years with SBS, which televises one live game a week, as well as two magazine shows and a highlights package, as well as bringing on board Foxtel who agreed to cover every game live in addition to other content. It's clear that the NSL could have commanded a higher fee for exclusive cable content, but the APSC wisely saw the difficulties that are emerging with Super Rugby in having no free-to-air content. Doubtless Foxtel were less perturbed about 'competing' with SBS in comparison to a commercial channel and perhaps this led to sharper pencils when the deals were signed. But in turn SBS has historically, culturally, emotionally and monetarily supported football and the ongoing relationship between the game and SBS is in many ways priceless and should continue to be nurtured. Finally, any inference that SBS is somewhere 'hard to find' on the dial or lacks profile was scotched a decade ago when Australia defeated Iran with record viewing ratings. If the product is good enough and desired enough, the punters will find it.

Promotion and relegation 2/10

An unresolved challenge for football in this country. The NSL is a closed league with no punishment for a poor finish on the table and (apart from expansion) no prospect for advancement from the current state leagues. Understandably, during this current phase of redevelopment NSL clubs need league and financial security but at some point, the league needs to resolve an issue that sets it apart from most of the football world.

The Women's National Soccer League 3/10

Professional women's football, particularly at national level, remains in its infancy in this country. But the 2000 Olympics surely planted the flag in Australia, announcing that the women's game is not only here to stay but is popular and will grow exponentially. We already see it at the grassroots level and we will continue to see it at international level. We got the first glimpses of this at the international level when the Matildas made the second stage at last year's World Cup for the first time. The WNSL, currently a part-time, limited competition, must be developed and grown as a matter of priority for the APSC.

Batsis finished his coffee and put the article down. *Not bad*, he thought. *Just a couple of things the team can clarify on Monday.* He went inside to see if the kids were ready.

Chapter 13

Sydney, Australia,

September 2008

Remo Nogarotto and Phil Moss gazed over the sprawling Macquarie University site and ran their visual rule on the ever-growing complex with satisfaction.

As the lease at North Sydney Oval finally expired at the end of the 2003–2004 season, Northern Spirit Football Club moved to Brookvale Oval. Deep down, Nogarotto was concerned that that pathway would almost surely lead to certain decline, tucked into a hard-to-get-to pocket on the Manly peninsula and trading a cricket oval for a bumpy rugby league pitch, hardly an improvement for a round ball to roll over. But the formation of the new league, the APSC's assistance, government and renewed financial investment, some lateral thinking and plain good fortune ultimately pointed the club in an entirely different direction.

The search for an alternate facility began as an exercise of literally putting pins into potential sites on a large wall map, hoping for a solution at the end of their agreed short tenure at Manly. Cromer Park was an option, as was Narrabeen Rugby Club on Pittwater Road, Valentine Park in the northwest, even Gordon Rugby's home ground in Chatswood. But all had significant challenges—difficulty with development, playing second fiddle to a primary user, difficulty with car parking or distance from public transport, or various combinations of these problems.

A chance meeting with Macquarie University's vice chancellor at a Sports Science dinner in 2006 was transforming. Remo had initially thought of delegating this to the team physio, but intuition told him to attend. The university was in fact looking for ways of expanding its nascent health sciences faculty and looking for investment and partnership opportunities. The vice chancellor was fairly football code agnostic but was acutely aware of the backgrounds of the majority of his overseas students, who were historically aligned to soccer and basketball rather than the rugby codes, cricket or AFL. To that end the two began discussing how a co-located football club and grounds could enhance the training, research and development of in particular sports science as well provide students, alumni and the local community with a national league level team to support.

There were other potential revenue benefits to the university. Revenue-raising food and beverage outlets operating under licence would have extended use during semester hours as well as on game days, with no effective competition for kilometres around. The entire space could become a social as well as a medical hub, much like the old showground site at Moore Park in Eastern Sydney had become.

The agreed location was a short walk and an even shorter drive from the ever-expanding university campus opposite. There were multiple ways that fans could get there. The site was easily accessible by car, via multiple motorway exits, from all corners of Northern Spirit's fan territory. Many local clubs across the region began looking at transporting kids and parents in hired buses on game day. And in time for next season, the Chatswood to Epping rail link would be completed with the new Macquarie University station providing public transport for those who preferred it.

Now, in time for the start of the new season, the final touches were being put on the shiny, compact new stadium. Following the cargo ships arriving, docking and unloading, the modular components had made their way on semi-trailers from Port Botany to Marsfield and had been painstakingly assembled over the winter. Each side had a cantilevered roof with the reinforced moulded behind-goal stands remaining open-ended.

Phil Moss oversaw a team that was responsible for the playing surface itself, as well as the layout of the secondary training ground and associated facilities. He had played at the club under Graham Arnold in the early days and joined the coaching staff as an assistant in 2002. Promotion to the top job had occurred last season when he steered the club to the semis for the first time in years. Now, finally, he would oversee the club being able to play on a manicured pitch and be able to truly demonstrate the passing and close control qualities of his charges.

But his contribution to the club went way beyond the roll of the ball.

From the start, both as a player and as a coach, Moss had made the squad available to local club gala days, federation nights and coaching clinics. Loyalty followed and in due course Northern Spirit had official relationships with the three enormous local federations of Kuringai, Manly Warringah and Gladesville-Hornsby. From Northbridge to Galston, from Avalon to Putney, Spirit had sewn up the entire swathe of Sydney football north of the harbour.

And it didn't stop there. Talks were already underway in the Central Coast area for Australia Cup games at Gosford Stadium, maybe even NSL fixtures there in due course. Northern Spirit could one day boast a geographical fan base stretching as far as 100 kilometres further north, all the way to Lake Macquarie.

All was in readiness for the visit of Adelaide United this coming Friday night for the season opener and around 9,000 fans were expected for the inaugural game at the now completed venue. The club had ditched the sky diving gimmick from North Sydney Oval long before, but there would be plenty of family-oriented stuff, from face painting to food stalls; the feeder leagues would have their junior teams on at half time and the 'Bush End Terrace' would be filled with the loyal active supporters. Many of the latter had been working tirelessly over the past two weeks painting banners and tifos with the assistance of the university's facilities.

***

Greater Sydney's other NSL teams, from the more traditional heartlands of the inner south and the western suburbs, looked on in disdain—and perhaps some jealousy—at the rise of the new 'silvertails' north of the Harbour Bridge.

Remo Nogarotto and his management team couldn't care less; they knew that the culture and territory they were developing was no different to other clubs around the world and merely represented the societal breadth of football across the planet. After all, every great football city had a team supported by the local 'well to do' and were often despised by others because of it. Turin had Juventus, Munich had Bayern, Porte Alegre Gremio and Buenos Aires had River Plate. Now, if Remo's management team had their way and things kept progressing, Sydney's equivalent would be Northern Spirit FC.

Chapter 14

Melbourne, Australia,

April 2009

The suburb of Sunshine was living up to its name on a cloudless autumn Sunday. The streets around Knights Stadium were congested to a standstill with car horns blaring, but mostly in celebration. All 20,000 tickets for the game that afternoon had been sold weeks ago and the scalpers were doing a brisk trade. The punters behind the goal were in full voice an hour before kick-off, and, in the fancy seats, the federal sports minister was being feted and would be part of the official grandstand naming ceremony just before the match itself. One TV news channel had even sent a helicopter for aerial pictures, and for once it wasn't to capture and play up an angle of 'soccer violence'. Even the visiting side Perth Glory was getting in on the atmosphere, despite being ten positions lower on the table and desperately needing a result from the fixture.

The fuss and excitement were appropriate. 'The Duke' was back in town.

Knights Stadium had been transformed over recent years. Now an all-seater with a new roof over the recently constructed sideline stand, its profile was nonetheless still dominated by the original edifice on the opposite side. The large imposing shed-like roof, alongside the new additions, gave the stadium an English championship side-like feel and the fans were right on top of the action. Given Lakeside's perimeter running track and Melbourne City's ongoing wait for the new Olympic Park to be completed, Knights supporters could rightly claim their ground to be the best football venue in Victoria.

In typical style, Mark Viduka had shunned a limousine ride to the game and insisted on driving himself, just like the rest of the squad. After all, he was staying at his parents' house at St Albans and it was only a short drive. "I'll get there in plenty of time, don't worry," he had advised the anxious event planner with a grin.

With more than a decade of European club football under his belt, a Socceroo captainship, and a veteran of two World Cups and two Olympic Games, 'Dukes' was football royalty and, as far as the Melbourne Knights were concerned, a deity. The president of the newly independent Croatia had come calling for him to represent the country of his ancestry in the 1990s, but Viduka had hitched his colours to Australia's mast, and few had any reason to doubt his loyalty. Like many Socceroos, he had busy and complete European club commitments year on year, often leading to missed early World Cup qualification rounds. But he never failed to disappoint when his country really needed him.

In many ways, Viduka represented the complex interplay between heritage and nationality that Australian soccer was, and how the game was now using this to full advantage as the NSL expanded in both geography and reach. The Melbourne Knights Football Club had, like many, begun as an important social and cultural hub for European migrants decades ago, in this case the Melbourne-based Croatian community. Their passion for identity and homeland independence ran deep, sometimes too deep for many. But a new century and a newly self-governed nation had coincided with a revitalised league, meaning the Knights could expand and flourish well beyond their original *raison-d'etre*.

There was plenty of heritage and hints of the ubiquitous red-and-white chequerboard, including on their crest, but the stands now consisted of fans and families from right across the northern suburbs of Melbourne and from right across the diverse cultural mix of modern Australia. Even when the occasional chant of "Cro-art-zia" boomed from behind the goal, young Australians of Asian to African background joined in the fun and only the vegetarians shunned the cevapi at half time.

Now it was time to formally honour and preserve in history the name of that most famous son of the Melbourne Knights with the unveiling of the Mark Viduka Stand, followed by the first of a three-game guest appearance.

***

The teams walked out onto the pitch to a raucous reception, accompanied by ceremonial music over the loudspeakers and red, white and blue banners carried by youngsters on the pitch itself. Somewhere, a flare erupted but was quickly extinguished. As the squads lined up on either side of the referees, the Melbourne Knights president and Minister Ellis called forth Viduka and in addressing the crowd officially bestowed the name 'Mark Viduka Stand' on the club's structure of pride and joy.

Given the emotions of the day with the one-sided and raucous crowd, the overawed Glory team and Viduka's enduring skill, it was no surprise that the game was one-way traffic. Perth had few goal-scoring opportunities with their attacking duo of Nikita Rukavytsya and James Robinson doing little to trouble the Knights keeper. In contrast, Viduka seemed to slot in seamlessly with the home side's young, impressive midfielder Marko Kuna and the more seasoned Robbie Kruse, newly signed from Brisbane Lions. An unanswered brace from Viduka and a third from Andrew Barasić sent the fans home in fine spirit. Given the game's free-to-air billing as the 'game of the round' and blanket news coverage across the channels, the match was a marketing and football masterstroke for both the national league and the Knights.

Guest appearances, final seasons 'at home' and official farewells were becoming popular across the NSL, particularly for those players who spent time in the league before heading overseas. What began as isolated decisions by individual clubs had now become formal APSC strategy, with the governing body making provision within their fighting funds that had also allowed for marquee signings. Visiting famous overseas players, often but not always at the end of their careers, provided glamour to the NSL and had been part of the Australian football landscape for decades. But returning Australian stars completed the full circle of local soccer's history. It was leading to a long overdue recognition of the game's past and as a result, also reflected the strength of the local game's continued potential for talent development. In due course, retiring great Australians would find their way into coaching and administrative positions that would ensure true football people had an active role in the game's future.

Chapter 15

Melbourne, Australia,

March 2010

The 'New Olympic Park' had finally been completed. From the first sod being turned, the whole affair had taken over three years. Investment from the Victorian and federal governments, the national rugby league and the NSL/APSC had resulted in a futuristic 30,000 capacity to be shared largely by Melbourne Storm and Melbourne City. Given the seasonal differences between the two competitions, there would be only modest overlap. It was hoped that appropriate curating would maintain an acceptable surface for both codes.

Outside of the ground itself, the precinct had been tarted up and connected with other nearby sporting venues.

As the final touches were being applied, the major hurdles became political and matters of history. Despite, it was rumoured, bitter protest behind the scenes from the AFL, the surprisingly more ecumenical Greek-descended state sports minister had agreed to the generic title of the Melbourne *Football* Stadium (MFS) for the venue. Deep down everyone knew that a sponsor's name would mask that in any event, but the name would at least shine through on ABC broadcast platforms and for World Cup qualifying or similar events.

Then there was the matter of grandstand naming. Both codes agreed to share out the stand names, but both codes' teams had little history to call upon. In soccer's case, most of the famous former Victorian participants of the game were rightly claimed by the city's other two national league clubs.

In the end, Soccer Australia's suggestion that the main eastern stand be called the Bresciano-Grella Stand won the day. Both players grew up and began their football careers in Victoria; they had performed with distinction through the 2000s for Australia and both had made guest appearances at Melbourne City towards the end of their respective careers. The southern end was named in honour of Bob Bignall, Australia's captain at the 1956 Melbourne Olympic Games. This was despite protests from a minority of parochial Victorians who objected that a New South Welshman should gain such an honour in their fair state.

Melbourne Storm were much more restricted in their options but ultimately settled upon the Cameron Smith Stand and the Geyer End.

The stadium was officially opened in March 2010 which conveniently meant that the Storm won the right to host the inaugural game on the new surface as their season opener. In contrast was City's first fixture there, the must-win tie against Adelaide to ensure the home team cemented their place in the finals.

The NSL side's inaugural game at the MFS was a boilover. Just shy of 20,000 were on hand to watch a high intensity soccer game with drama both on and off the pitch.

The game began in pedestrian fashion, with both teams understandably anxious not to concede a goal early. John Kosmina, enjoying his second spell as Adelaide coach, had assembled a no-nonsense team both in midfield and defence, but with just enough flair up front. They certainly weren't there just to make up the numbers and took the game right up to Melbourne, hoping to spoil the opening party. Progressively, an element of niggle began to take over with the tackles becoming increasingly aggressive and at times reckless. Four yellow cards were issued in 20 minutes at the back end of the first half alone. On 40 minutes, Adelaide defender Robbie Cornthwaite brought down Archie Thompson inside the box and the referee pointed straight to the spot. Angry scuffles broke out but, when the dust settled, Thompson converted in front of the red and white legion and City went to the sheds 1–0 up.

Regardless of what might have been said in the dressing rooms by the respective managers, the fuse had been lit for the second half. The game was now at a frenetic pace and when Sergio van Dyke rounded City defender Simon Colosimo to equalise from a through ball that seemed inches offside, the entire City squad, including the bench, launched themselves verbally at both the referee and his assistants. Amidst the argy-bargy, more cards, including a red, were dispensed and the goal ultimately stood.

It didn't stop there. In the 54th minute, City captain Kevin Muscat chased a ball over the sideline, careered into Kosmina on the Adelaide bench, and sent him tumbling over backwards. Kosmina stood up and immediately grabbed Muscat by the throat, leading to his sending from the bench to the stands. Muscat earned the game's ninth yellow.

Finally, with five minutes to spare, Melbourne forward John Aloisi picked up the ball 20 metres out, got the better of Boogard, and lashed home into the bottom left-hand corner of the net, striking a dagger into the club of his home city.

Full time sounded and the pushing and shoving on the pitch continued. Travelling Adelaide fans traded verbal barbs with their rivals but were outnumbered and outsung by the locals, who partied well into the evening with only minor indiscretions reported.

The Melbourne Football Stadium had been well and duly christened.

***

One week later, Melbourne City found themselves just a few kilometres from home in a derby against South Melbourne that would determine the last of the upcoming finals positions. Lakeside had been sold out on the Monday prior.

Arriving at the precinct, fans filed past the famous statue of Ferenc Puskas that had been lovingly restored and relocated outside the main entrance from the MFS construction area. It was now finally in a position of prominence, duly honouring one of the most famous strikers in football history and his time as the coach of South Melbourne from 1989 to 1991. From there, the punters entered the recently refashioned combined athletic and football arena which now very much resembled a middle European venue, with a curved roof reminiscent of the Ullevi Stadium in Gothenburg. Seating alterations and additions meant the facility could comfortably accommodate 20,000 patrons.

The upgraded Trimboli End was full to overflowing 90 minutes before kickoff, whilst the fortunate holders of tickets to the fancy seats in the Postecoglou Stand could take their time in the grandstand's eateries and bars before assuming their positions.

South Melbourne Football Club liked to claim Victorian football royalty status for themselves and with some justification. The club had celebrated its 50th anniversary the year before and had progressively evolved from their original Hellenic roots to that of a perennial powerhouse of the NSL. Earlier in the year the club was officially recognised as Oceania club of the 20th century.

Their history, cultural roots and football philosophy had no greater expression than in their favourite protege Ange Postecoglou. The son of Greek migrants, he would go on to play with distinction for his club in addition to representing his country, as well as successfully coach South to multiple titles. Postecoglou's club coaching career culminated in an admirable performance on the world stage at the FIFA Club World Championship in 2000. Now, after rising through the national coaching ranks, he was about to lead Australia to its fourth World Cup appearance in a few months' time.

In bright autumn sunshine the hosts dominated a skilful and free-flowing encounter that contrasted the tantrums of the week before, South running out 3–1 victors including two sublime efforts from Marco Rojas, signed earlier in the season from Christchurch United, who had entered the league the season before. The active fans carried the day with their sounds and colour, the older heads nodded and applauded, and football, as they often say, was the real winner.

***

Sydney Olympic might have been premiers for the season and odds-on favourite for the grand final, but the preceding two weeks had belonged to Victorian football. Melbourne football clubs could trace their roots back to the late 19th century, with a strong British background that was infused vibrantly through migration after the Second World War. They were co-founders of the national league in the 1970s and were battle-hardened through their endless struggles against Australian Rules football's determination to deny them social and cultural presence, medial space and even facilities for local park games. But now they had firmly planted their stake in 21st century Victoria and south of the Murray, the game would never look back.

The completion and integration of the Melbourne Football Stadium was the last piece in the jigsaw puzzle of the National Stadium Project. Combined with existing state facilities, construction works from Brisbane to Sydney to Canberra to Christchurch had resulted in standalone boutique grounds—soccer-friendly facilities to match the league's various clubs across Australasia. The NSL could look forward to a high intensity finals series and a grand final in a suitable venue, both in the current season and for years to come. And for the nation, another World Cup appearance after another successful qualification was just around the corner.

Chapter 16
Durban, South Africa,
June 2010

The meeting officially wound up and Kimon Taliadoros exchanged some light conversation, then left through the hotel lobby towards Durban's expansive beach. Like the day before it, it had been a long one, and some fresh sea air was in order.

It had, however, been a successful couple of days where Soccer Australia's strategic aims had been achieved and in turn, the Oceania Confederation's administration and football direction strengthened and ratified.

Just 42 years of age, Taliadoros' rise through football, both on and off the pitch, had been stellar. After over 200 appearances for a number of NSL clubs (in particular South Melbourne) and nine appearances for Australia, Taliadorios served firstly as a founding executive member and then ultimately president of the Professional Players' Association in the 1990s. His experience and administrative skills were too significant for football to let him out of its grasp and, following several successful business roles, he was a natural fit for the administrative hole that Soccer Australia had found itself in by the mid-2000s. Board membership of the reconstituted body was followed by chairmanship in 2008, taking over from Les Avory who had filled the position since Hill's departure in 2003.

Taliadoros had overseen the implementation of the strategic plan Soccer Australia had introduced some years earlier. That included taking a more central role in the administration of Oceania, helping the confederation to reform its processes from top down, providing key advisors and committee memberships, assisting the Pacific nations with football administration more generally and ensuring that FIFA provided more development funding.

And of course, to ensure that Oceania's qualification play-off pathway continued to be through the Asian Football Confederation.

On the eve of the 2010 World Cup, with a newly recognised credibility across the game, he and his team had just successfully navigated the various subcommittees and ultimately the FIFA Congress itself. A regional annual trans-Pacific club event, the *O League*, as well as formalised youth and women's tournament pathways, were all ratified. Most importantly, as long as the World Cup remained a 32-team event, Congress voted that Oceania's playoff route was via Asia.

The mid-winter air was cold but invigorating as Kimon looked out at the ocean. He thought about the Australian squad preparing for the tournament in Johannesburg. It was time to turn the attention back to the pitch, the Socceroos meeting Slovakia in Rustenburg in just a few days' time.

***

Despite a strategically polished performance in what was now clearly Postecoglou's playing style, the Socceroos failed to get out of their group. They started brightly enough against Slovakia but failed to convert their chances, the game ending scoreless. In contrast, Paraguay created a boilover by defeating a hesitant Italian team 2–0. The reigning world champions found themselves immediately at the bottom of their group and needing to bounce back quickly.

Four days later, the Socceroos met the *Azzuri* in Nelspruit in another tight encounter. The Australians took an early lead through a headed goal from Kennedy, who latched on to a superb cross from Luke Wilkshire. In the midfield, Mile Jedinak and Vince Grella seemed to have the measure of an ageing Andrea Pirlo and his midfield compatriots, but on 58 minutes the Italians, against the run of play, it was generally agreed, restored parity when the experienced Mauro Camoranesi put Antonio Di Natale clean through on goal with Schwarzer unable to do anything.

With ten minutes remaining, the Italian substitute Fabio Quagliarella evaded Grella deep on the left side of the field and sprinted into the 18-metre area with the ball at his feet. He clattered into Jedinak and tumbled spectacularly to the ground. Australian hearts were in mouths, rightly so when replays were later analysed, but the referee waved play on. The Italians were incensed at what they saw as complete injustice; they promptly surrounded the official with gesticulations and what seemed like outright threats. Two were booked and play resumed, but the score line finished 1–1.

That left both Australia and Italy needing wins from their final group games against Paraguay and Slovakia respectively. It was a chance for the Socceroos to exact revenge for their qualification elimination eight years earlier, but the South Americans were simply too good. A 40th minute goal was unanswered as Paraguay proceeded to a second three points and to top the group.

Australia departed the tournament with only two points, exiting along with the Italians. The *Azzuri* were generally unimpressive and, despite their dour 1–0 win over Slovakia in their final group game, were eliminated by the central Europeans on goal difference.

Despite the disappointment, Australians were becoming accustomed to regular World Cup appearances and stopping as a nation to follow the Socceroos' exploits. The dark years after 1974 were becoming a distant memory and, for many younger fans, that era existed only in the history books. The press, rightly or wrongly, started to regard World Cup appearances by the Socceroos as a *fait accompli*, although the purists wished there was a little more media savvy when it came to a discussion of tactics and the ongoing development of the game. Additionally, at home it seemed that at last, after more than 30 years, there was a viable, stable national league of good quality.

There was consensus that both domestically and internationally, 2010 was a transformative and watershed year for the Australian game.

Chapter 17

Newcastle, Australia,

December 2010

After a week's labour, Friday afternoon had come at last and for the football faithful of Newcastle, this meant a quick stop at the local pub before heading up to the International Sports Centre (ISC) for an important fixture against South Melbourne. Christmas was only a week away and given the Newcastle Jet's tepid midfield of late and their mid-table position, the home fans were hoping for a performance that matched the progressively rising temperature that came with the year's end.

With a deep passion for football and its history at both club and national level, foremost amongst those fans was David McGaw.

David was football personified. He had played as a youngster and had watched and followed with excitement as Newcastle KB United entered the National Soccer League in the second season in 1978. They had been heady times. United had been a runaway sensation in the soccer-mad city, drawing massive crowds. As a youngster, David's attendance had been limited, as his father had seen game day as the one chance each week to have a beer with his mates, unencumbered by small fry to watch over. But to this day, McGaw the younger could name a result on any given weekend and in particular the precise day when the KB United franchise had collapsed in 1984. A brief respite had occurred when Adamstown Rosebud stepped in, literally overnight, to keep a NSL team alive for the city over the next two years. Sadly, their best efforts hadn't been able to financially sustain the enterprise and, for an unconscionable five seasons, the city with the finest of football pedigrees was bereft of top flight soccer.

Enter Adamstown's rival Newcastle Austral, a multicultural outfit who had created and administered the Newcastle Breakers as the city's NSL team for much of the 1990s.

Fans like McGaw had seen the greater order of things: that irrespective of background support and northern New South Wales rivalry, the important thing for Newcastle and the country was to have a team from his city playing at the highest level. The Breakers, in the opinion of many locals, had been tarred with the Austral brush, but they had plied their trade admirably in a national league that chopped and changed through much of the decade.

David took it all in, and, like many fans, the overlapping backdrop of the national team's performance had its own prominence to him. The Socceroos' recurring failures had come to a head during the home-and-away fixture against Iran in November 1997. McGaw had watched the return leg from home on television, uncertain as to the outcome until the tumultuous national anthem and the frenetic first half, at which point he had dared to believe the unbelievable. He had simultaneously rejoiced and wept as the game concluded in a victory that saw the end of a 24-year World Cup absence and he had hastily booked his trip to France.

That had been over a decade ago, in which time he had changed careers from a greenkeeper to his higher calling of teacher; and during which time the fair city of Newcastle went through yet another football evolution.

When the Breakers had stumbled at the end of the decade, it was the newly formed Newcastle United's turn to fly the city's flag. Financed predominantly by businessman David Hall, United had faced the same challenges that all the previous iterations had. Despite significant local media support and in-principle endorsement from the punters, falling crowd support and financial distress had smelt strongly of history, sadly, repeating itself.

McGaw had been sanguine about the whole exercise. His personal view had always been that the city and its people just didn't have it in them for sustained national competition representation under a traditional top-down business ownership model. Whether it was football, the basketball team or even the 'mighty' Newcastle Knights Rugby League team, without artificial propping up all would have already folded, or fold in due course. Which was why the Newcastle Jets that emerged phoenix-like from the ashes was not only satisfying but inspiring and a model for the rest of football across the country.

When in the fullness of time David Hall's financial support began to waver, there had been an ill wind right across the nation for the National Soccer League. During the 2002/2003 season it hadn't been just about Newcastle's means of survival; the future of the entire NSL was at stake. Hall had had enough and wanted out: the question was, who would replace him and what would be the best way to develop a model that wouldn't just keel over within five years?

The uncertainty around ownership had coincided with the formation of the APSC. Suddenly there had been a flurry about external investment, ground development and, in Newcastle at that time, there had been a new potential investor in the loyal and well-meaning Con Constantine. But running a fully professional club would cost millions per year and for a city the size of Newcastle, that would always be challenging. Furthermore, there would be no appetite for again turning to an existing club like Adamstown to fill the space, as this would inevitably alienate other fans in the city. Better that the good football fans of Newcastle could keep their local regional team as well as jointly and secondarily worshipping at the ecumenical temple of the Jets.

Enter a group of local businessmen, community figures and former players, including Ray Baartz and Craig Johnston, with a proposal that they had stated was always in front of everyone's faces, albeit a long way from home, successful in many parts of Europe. A community ownership model.

The best example was in Spain. FC Barcelona, Catalonia's sporting religion, had been owned by the fans for decades using the Spanish *soci* model. For a hundred or so euros a year, over 100,000 fans have maintained membership in what remains a private registered club. In return, the members get to speak and vote on important club edicts as well as approve things like the club's financials. They also had access to discounted tickets and, given they comprised a majority of the 90,00-plus gate at Camp Nou on match day, go by the nickname the *cules* ('bums'), although in fairness there were other historical origins of that term.

Then there was the Bundesliga federation-dictated ownership model in Germany, the so-called '50+1' principle, which had been in operation since 1998. Under this principle, members own 50 percent of their clubs plus one share, limiting commercial investment to a minority stake. The principle ensures that members can directly influence off-field matters because they always own a majority stake in the club.

What the Newcastle luminaries were proposing was a hybrid of the various European models in a way they felt would suit the local landscape.

The final formula, for the first season, was fairly black and white. Constantine invested three million dollars which was determined to be 40 percent of the reformed club's baseline startup requirements of seven and a half million. From there, it was planned that around 10,000 fans would each be willing to pay a subscription of just under ten dollars a week, or five hundred dollars a year. They would receive voting rights for off-field matters, including directorships in the private unlisted company, as well as heavily discounted tickets to each Jets home game.

In addition to a voice in the company's direction and finances, investing fans would progressively receive shares for each $1,000 they committed. There were no plans to actually float the company on the stock exchange and goodness knew if a surplus would ever be paid to the investors. More likely any leftover change would be re-invested into the club. But there was the emotional bond of knowing *"I own a football club!"*

As the model developed, other benefits were approved. The mid-north coast *culés* got to have a say when it came to marquee players or returning Socceroo guest appearances. At the other end of player engagement, in an uncommon display of NSL-State Federation unity, investor families were given heavily discounted access to the new regional youth academy that the Jets were instrumental in developing with the Northern New South Wales Federation. This was designed to overcome the problem of talented youngsters from less wealthy families being unable to access skills development and progression in the game.

In due course, this fledgling relationship with the Northern New South Wales Federation at Edgeworth was envisaged to lead to the Jets housing their training facilities and administration there. And who knew, maybe one day a stadium of their own at the facility.

David was, of course, a year one investor, although he had little time to worry about the tin tacks. He was delighted to at last have a stable, well-performing team in his hometown and it was just a happy coincidence that in some small way, he was structurally part of it. After all, away from Jets games, he had lessons to prepare and an overlarge backyard to which he could apply his greenkeeper's skills.

But for the next couple of hours, he could take his seat at the ISC and indulge in his favourite pastime.

Chapter 18

Sydney, Australia,

June 2011

Andre Kruger eased off the accelerator of his second-hand Golf GTI. It was easy to speed along the F6 motorway, especially once north of Mount Ousley, and he was still getting used to the fact that unlike the German *autobahns*, there were significant penalties for exceeding the speed limit on similar roads in Australia. But the Australian football afficionado, collector of memorabilia and Soccer Hall of Fame recipient was genuinely excited as he headed towards his meeting at St George Stadium with Soccer Australia and his long-term hero, now firm friend, Rale Rasić. After all, the meeting was to finally confirm the realisation of their jointly held dream: the establishment of an Australian football museum.

He continued into suburban Sydney, past St George Hospital, and through the back streets to the stadium. Andrew Hatzionannou, Sydney Olympic's number one fan, season ticket holder and presently front gate man for the club's facilities, flashed that famous toothy smile as he recognised Kruger and waved him through.

The complex had grown significantly since the heady amateur days of the 1980s, when a single stand on the western side watched over a pitch that was otherwise surrounded by grassed embankments. In those days, St George–Budapest had ruled the roost there, but the ground had also seen World Cup qualifiers and even a visit from Pelé. But a new era, new tenants and the National Stadium Project had seen the site transformed.

The ground was now fully surrounded by seating, with roofing over the eastern and western sides. A second training field and facilities along with Olympics' administrative offices on the western side were all completed a couple of years ago. The final roofing to complete the 25,000 all-seater stadium over the behind-goal ends was due within two years. Along with the likes of Marconi and the Melbourne Knights, these transforming club homes were the jewels in the crown of a strategy that successfully combined the proceeds of private investment, government money and television revenue. They left other sporting codes shaking their heads as to the ingenuity and cost effectiveness of their design and build.

***

Andre carefully scrutinised the proposed space underneath the eastern stand of St George Stadium. Originally trained as a draftsman, for many years Andre had developed significant expertise in the management of commercial property space. He had a keen eye for issues such as electricity supply, fire safety and security. There was still much work to be done before any precious cargo could be safely housed here but certainly there was sufficient space. Olympic were planning to offer them an area of around 70m x 20m, with the arching roof space above for any large hung items.

With the tour completed, the guests sat down for their meeting to sort out the nitty-gritty. Present were Andre and Rale Rasić, along with Mike Brown from the Soccer Australia Board, Francis Awaritefe representing the Professional Players' Association, and Michael Darvos, the newly appointed CEO of Sydney Olympic.

"Well, what do you think?" asked Michael, after the initial pleasantries were done with. "It would be an honour for our club and our stadium to house the museum."

"There's been so much talking, talking for many years about a proper football museum, so it's fantastic to finally be able to realise that dream," said Andre in his German-accented English. He glanced down at the floor plans. "Obviously there are many details still to be sorted out, including appropriate flooring and lighting, alarms and many things, but there's enough room. Thanks to Soccer Australia for helping to fund the project. With their permission, I'd be very happy to take on the role as curator and part-time manager of the museum and help the Federation with things like layout and different display sections."

Andre knew that however keen he was, the museum would not get off the ground unless people like Rale Rasić were absolutely confident as to the security and tenure of the museum contents. After all, a significant proportion of the collection would come from Rasić's own personal treasure trove developed over many years, not only from his role as coach of the Australian 1974 World Cup side but also through his vast personal connections across the football community worldwide. His extensive collection ranged from jerseys to signed mementos to document cabinets full of printed articles from around the soccer world. It was all lovingly housed and presently cared for in his purpose-built sheds at the back of his house in the western suburbs of Sydney. But it wasn't just Rasić; if former Socceroos and their families were to donate or loan precious items that they or their family members had secured during their years in the game, it was vital that the museum was established in a way that could guarantee safety and storage quality.

Andre said aloud, "Obviously everything has to be on the utmost safety and security as there are many things that have gone missing from Australia's football history. Who knows where they are now?" He also thought of his own collection, mostly still in safekeeping in Germany. How to securely transport it here? Then he foresaw months of contacting players and their families across the country, negotiations, contracts, insurance. On site, there would be much work and expense required with glass cabinetry, framing of items, arranging, and safely displaying or hanging.

Finally, there would be extensive cataloguing and the creation of an online wing of the museum.

There was discussion amongst the group as to the proportionate attention to the NSL as opposed to the national teams within the displays. Brown and Darvos agreed that a section for the national league was warranted. "After all," said Darvos, who was also representing the APSC, "the two are intrinsically connected in Australian football history. It was the performance of the 1974 Socceroos in West Germany that led to the establishment of the National Soccer League all the way back in '77."

The Federation and the Players' Association had many connections with respect to NSL memorabilia and Soccer Australia still had possession of items such as the old Ampol Cup, contested in the past by teams from New South Wales. They discussed general plans for a display that encompassed the inauguration, history and teams that had variously been part of the NSL over the years.

When it came to the national men's teams, Andre had already made plans. Each section would feature an Australian captain representing a particular era, from the Australian Cap number one Alex Gibb from

1922, or the '56 Olympics, through to Wilson (of course), leading ultimately to the modern era's World Cup captains: Alex Tobin, Mark Viduka and Lucas Neill. Within each section there would be memorabilia, jerseys, multimedia presentations, trophies, banners and flags. But to pull all of that together there was a need for signage, explanations, thoroughfares that led visitors along those timelines.

There would be much to do, but to Andre Kruger, relatively speaking, it would be nothing but an absolute labour of love. His life's calling had come at last.

Chapter 19

Zurich, Switzerland,

October 2011

Ange Postecoglou sat through the entire global qualification draw for the 2014 World Cup, with as best a level gaze as he could. Amongst his national team coaching colleagues, especially from Europe, there was always the murmured excitement from the audience as the second and top seeded European teams came out of the bowls towards the end of the draw, but for the Pacific it would be same old same old. After all, the Oceania Confederation's World Cup qualification pathway was painfully repeatable and was always first up. After some preliminaries, two groups of the better teams from the region would be established, keeping Australia and New Zealand apart, of course. Those two groups would play home and away to determine the top team from each group, who would then play off over two legs to determine who would face the fifth best team from Asia.

Whilst there were now a spattering of Pacific Island players in the NSL, interest in them was only modest when it came to representing their country. In fact, the only real debating point at the early phase of any qualification cycle was whether Tim Cahill would turn out for Samoa, and whether Australia ended up on that side of the draw.

Cahill's story felt like so many of those of Socceroo aspirants who had gone before him, wanted in vain by the Australian Federation and the football public to turn out for the national team. However, in reality, his journey was so very different to the likes of Craig Johnston or Tony Dorigo.

Born in Sydney, his football skills, discipline and sheer determination shone early in local club football, and he was quickly established in England playing professionally for Millwall as the Socceroos were gearing up for *France '98*. However, as requests for international duty came to him from more than one front, it was on the opposite side of the planet that Cahill's international fate had already been cast four years earlier at the age of 14, when he debuted for Western Samoa, coming on as a substitute in a 3–0 loss to New Zealand.

As his international star began to shine ever more brightly, his appearances for the Samoan youth team, from FIFA's perspective, were locked in. Any representation at international level, even in the junior ranks, meant that the player in question was forever tied to that nation. But across the planet there was growing disquiet at what appeared on the surface to be a harsh rule, especially for young players. How could a teenager, particularly one with multiple backgrounds, be expected to make a definitive decision about national duty when so young and with so much incentive from different sources?

Keen for him to play for Australia, national coach Frank Farina, with Soccer Australia's backing, took up Cahill's case to FIFA, as one of a number of 'test cases' around the globe, hoping to rectify what was a glaring anomaly. The eventual ruling upholding the status quo was a bitter blow for many, foremost amongst them Tim Cahill.

The Australian media berated Soccer Australia for not "doing more" but, in reality, the die was cast through the powerful African Confederation. Keen to develop their own national team stocks and arguing that their federations nurtured talent for the future betterment of their member nations, Africa, particularly paranoid about the talent drain the continent was experiencing to Europe, lobbied hard for the existing situation to remain. The nations of three other confederations also jumped on board. As a result, a majority at FIFA Congress voted in support of the current rule remaining.

Cahill turned his attention to rising through the ranks of the English Premier League with Everton and Chelsea, a living example that everything and everyone in football is beholden to FIFA's politics.

But to his credit, he never forgot his roots. In the 21st century as FIFA progressively aligned international breaks from club football across the globe, Cahill would return to appear for Samoa for important World Cup qualifiers. A 1–1 draw with Australia in Sydney in 2009 was marked by a trademark goal from a header as he rose above defenders seemingly twice his height. Directly and indirectly, his legacy for the entire Oceania football region was significant.

***

The draw completed—and for the record with Samoa landing on New Zealand's side—Postecoglou made a brief appearance at the post-draw function. He wanted to get home and had lots of planning to do. With the *golden generation* now very much in the rear-view mirror, he was starting to become anxious as to the depth of the Socceroos' squad for the upcoming qualification series. He had some serious planning and recruiting to do.

Chapter 20
Sydney, Australia,
March 2013

Pablo Bateson arrived at Soccer Australia headquarters punctually and, after some niceties over coffee, took his seat at the Annual Congress Meeting. After years of political to-ing and fro-ing, the occasional firm nudge from FIFA, and above all, a recognition that Australia was at risk of losing many of its newly found executive appointments with the Oceania Federation if it didn't get its act together, the much-maligned National Congress was born. It was not so much fine-tuned but cobbled together by all of the noisy self-interested parties that in theory represented the Australian football landscape.

The biggest dinosaurs of all were, of course, the state federations. New South Wales even had two federations for good measure. Just like railway track gauges, geographical sporting code differences and multiple replicated government bureaucracies, the state federations were those structures that were forged in Australia's colonial past. It was always hard to believe, on encountering this kind of state-based relics, that the country had ever federated at all.

The triple decker of governments federal, state and local council, the natural outcome of a large land-mass country with a small population, meant that the nation was gloriously over governed. It appeared that Soccer Australia almost took pride in imitating the national tolerance of excessive administration, or at least that story did a good job of hiding the fact that a flatter, more cost-efficient corporate structure was simply in the way-too-hard basket.

Having sat down, Pablo leaned back and resisted a wince as he hit against the back of his chair. One week later, he was still recovering from his sunburn and was angry at himself for getting into trouble in the first place. After a near death medical experience a few years ago, he prided himself that no matter where his travels took him, some basic medical self-preservation and common sense would ensure ongoing good health.

Sadly, he had let himself down with respect to both last week in Honiara. The Green and Gold Army, the national teams' official supporters group, had arranged a fundraising game of beach football with some locals. A couple of beers, followed by joining the 'skins' side, meant that only 15 minutes of near equatorial sun was enough to leave Pablo red raw from the waist up.

That aside, the latest Green and Gold Army Pacific tour was popular and well attended. This one was termed the 'Melanesian Swing' as the supporters group followed the Socceroos' away games to Fiji and the Solomon Islands. Victories were effectively guaranteed but fans of all persuasions and means enjoyed the tours immensely. There was a choice between a week's resort stay at the Fiji Intercontinental with a round at the nearby championship golf course thrown in, south of the game venue in Nadi; or alternatively, more modest digs just outside the main town with appropriate nightly entertainment. Either way, the first part of the tour had something for all comers. A Pacific connection to Honiara for the second game wasn't everyone's cup of tea, but for the young and enthusiastic a reef surfing add-on in the

Solomons was something not to be missed.

In both countries, community-minded fans like Bateson were keen to connect with the locals and, through charities, help them along. The latter didn't figuratively lead to Pablo losing his shirt by any means—if only he had actually physically kept it on, when it mattered most.

Immediately after the second international, Pablo left the surfers to it and headed home. The tour was a roaring success and, on the park, as expected, the Socceroos were undefeated on top of Oceania Phase 2, Group A with home games to follow shortly.

Many fans and administrators constantly cursed the fact that Australia, who saw herself as a better-than-middle-grade world football power, seemed to be rooted in the backwaters of Oceania forever. It meant a dearth of real international football for a significant proportion of the four-year World Cup cycle. But in reality, the soccer world was slowly but surely evolving. Friendly matches across confederations were becoming increasingly like hen's teeth, as particularly Europe withdrew into itself and created more UEFA competitions that swamped that continent's calendar.

In Asia, where Australia had once desperately but rather arrogantly wanted to join for so long in the past, there seemed to only be four or five truly high-grade teams anyway. Much of that confederation's qualification process, like Oceania's, consisted of unbalanced games against minnows, particularly in the early qualification rounds. In any event, thanks to Soccer Australia's rare show of negotiating strength back in 2010, the Oceania champions now played an Asian team in the World Cup Confederation playoffs rather than one from South America. Combined with a spot at the Confederations Cup for the Oceania Champions, on balance, the Socceroos weren't too badly off for meaningful games and the chance for advancement.

Additionally, there were clear advantages at youth, women's and

Olympic levels where the island-centred 'baby brother' confederation continued to enjoy direct qualification.

For the fans, tour organisers and supporter groups now had a plethora of offerings for not only the 'big time' events, especially the World Cup itself, but also to idyllic locations from Noumea to Raratonga. And from there, later to exotic places like Muscat, Tashkent or Hanoi. What wasn't there to like?

* * *

The meeting droned on, and Pablo's back soreness at least ensured that he maintained his focus. As head of the Australian Football Supporter's Group and therefore holding the hard-won singular fan position on Congress, it was vital that he represented and stood up for the people whom the game surely was really all about—the fans. Those people who played as youngsters, later put up nets and cooked sausages at their local clubs and in due course rusted themselves onto their professional club as well as their country. Without them, turnstiles wouldn't turn, broadcast deals wouldn't be struck and players' wages wouldn't be paid.

It was an ongoing debate as to whom professional football should be most beholden to. Bateson had read that at Harvard Business School, students were taught to distinguish a 'customer focused' organisation from a 'employee focused' one when it came to strategic planning. Administrators and players across the globe always considered football to be the latter, but the fans, along with knowledgeable journalists, considered otherwise.

Eventually, Pablo was up. After the Congress had spent hours wrangling about everything from player contract status and registration fee levels across the country to revenue splits between the National Soccer League and the Federation, he had limited time to try to bring the Congress up to speed and lobby for his group's cause.

Forged out of an uneasy truce of the various active supporter groups across the country, the Australian Football Supporter's Group—or AFSG as it was more commonly known—had a tough task more akin to herding warfaring cats. But gradually, progress had been made.

In recent years, some genuine crowd trouble had been met by heavy-handedness from private security guards and state police. Sadly, this had evolved into over-responsiveness at any perceived 'soccer unrest' which in turn led to a backlash from the more active supporter groups. Everything from standing on seats—or even just standing—through to confiscation of banners and 'excessive language' was met with evictions and bans. The situation risked getting out of hand and also risked the atmosphere and crowds at the NSL. After all, active support was a key difference at soccer compared to other football codes and was a chief source of attraction of young people to NSL fixtures.

There was also an increasing recognition that active fans were part of the game day entertainment for other 'non-active' fans. They provided a fantastic backdrop for both broadcasting and news items and should be encouraged. At a recent Olympic–Marconi sold-out derby at St George Stadium, *The Daily Telegraph* sent a senior rugby league journalist to record decibel levels at each end.

With the founding of AFSG the representatives of most active fan groups met with the new entity to begin positive dialogue. It took some time for inherent biases to be put aside, to achieve progress, and to move towards common goals. In turn, the parent body became a properly constituted entity with appropriate governance, audited financials and a formal meeting structure. Pablo Bateson, with his history of active support, fan advocacy and football writing was the obvious choice for chairman of the group.

AFSG was officially recognised within the NSL administration and in due course gained formal recognition and admission to Soccer Australia's Congress. But the appointment to the latter was largely a token one and generally treated in patronising overtones by the Federation. It was against this difficult backdrop that Pablo sought to now receive the go-ahead, along with money, to institute a policy not only for the NSL but across all levels of the game.

"Members of Congress, thank you for giving me the opportunity to update you as to our recent activities. You may know that Australian Football Supporters Group now represents the fan groups of thirteen NSL clubs."

"Not everyone?" asked Ben Gordonson, one of the more vocal State Federation presidents and known for his antipathy towards fans.

"That's something we are working on, but the overwhelming majority. We also represent a number of fan groups at state league level. We are also recognised," Pablo added as he glanced across at the APSC representatives, "by the APSC with whom we have a good working relationship."

He allowed this to sit for a moment.

Pablo continued. "Over the last two years we have been working hard with the APSC, particularly with respect to active support and over policing. The heavy-handedness of security guards and police at NSL matches, often in completely unwarranted circumstances, has had a detrimental effect on both atmosphere and crowds. The NSL's administration recognised that a proactive relationship could achieve common goals. For example, that standing and coordinated noise are appropriate, but flares not. That tifos are an important part of the atmosphere, but so is visible advertising."

Gordonson retorted, "Are you suggesting, Pablo, that you have eliminated all problems? I would suggest that everyone knows of recent examples of ongoing trouble." This was a direct if underhanded reference to some recent crowd skirmishes, flares and arrests at the home matches at one or two older clubs.

"Of course not," Pablo replied. "Nor are we suggesting that perfection will ever be achieved. But the alternative is unfettered security and police presence left unchecked, with adverse consequences to crowd numbers and gate takings."

After a moment, Pablo continued. "We are not arguing for no rule of law, nor for self-policing. Instead, fans groups should be self-regulating. Unacceptable behaviours will not be accepted and individuals expressing those views or acting in inappropriate ways will be excluded. In turn, the recognised leaders of the fan groups warrant to act in a responsible way and maintain a good relationship with club administration."

"This sounds like a very fine utopia, Pablo!" Ben replied sarcastically.

Pablo was tiring of the negativity but chose not to bite. "It works pretty well across most of western Europe. So, what we have begun successfully with the Association of Professional Soccer Clubs, we would like to formalise through Soccer Australia, with policy and funding. I trust you all have read the proposal that I have circulated to all Congress members ahead of today."

The Congress Chair was keen to wrap this up. "Yes, we have, and thank you very much for your time, Pablo. Representatives of the various stakeholder groups will read your documentation and we can discuss this further in the near future."

"So, there is no case for further discussion and some decisions today?" Pablo was getting exasperated.

"Unfortunately not, as we are well behind time with a very full agenda. But thanks again, Pablo. We'll get back to you." With that, the Congress moved to the next agenda item.

Pablo, angry and frustrated, and sick of his damn sunburn, stood and walked out. *So much for a recognition of the fans,* he fumed to himself as he left the building.

Chapter 21

Melbourne, Australia,

October 2013

The full-time whistle sounded, leading off a chorus of boos that rang around the Melbourne Football Stadium. The Australian players, with various emotional combinations of anger, frustration and disbelief, stood with their hands on their hips or fell to the turf. In contrast, the entire Kiwi squad congregated as the bench swept onto the pitch, progressively smothered and gathered their on-field players and sprinted towards their supporters behind the southern goal in pure celebration.

Ange Postecoglou had an expression more akin to an Easter Island statue as he stood alone on the sideline, before slowly striding onto the pitch to variously congratulate the opposition and console his players.

What could possibly have gone wrong? How had the Socceroos let a golden chance to qualify for a fifth World Cup slip through their fingers, and embarrassingly only at the penultimate phase?

The Australian fans and media had some pretty good ideas.

Tactically, Ange was a master coach with a strategic style of play that demanded the best of his charges. The strategy of a high press, moving the ball amongst the team at pace, almost never backward and always playing out from the back, rather than a hoof upfield by the keeper, were all applauded by the fans. But even as Australia was sweeping aside the island nations, Postecoglou knew that his team needed to develop a style that could match it with teams far more accomplished.

In particular, he was obsessed with midfield dominance and instituted a back three system of defence. It was this approach that the Kiwis had successfully unpicked and had punished the home side, especially in the second leg in Victoria.

The problem was, thanks to limited Oceania World Cup qualifiers, that over the preceding two years the Australian squad had met infrequently, at one point not for more than a year. Players far flung from Europe and Asia were expected to drop their ingrained style at their respective clubs and somehow adapt to Postecoglou's new system with perhaps one or two training sessions only, alongside Socceroo teammates they rarely saw and barely knew.

Many fans and journalists felt this grand vision would come unstuck at some point. They had just hoped it would be in the group stages of *Brazil 2014*, not before. There was a widely held view that Postecoglou should have adopted a more traditional style that the team could efficiently integrate. Further, they considered that his playing philosophy was better suited to club football where he could oversee and steer a squad week on week and in a setting where games weren't one-off do-or-die affairs.

For Postecoglou, this was likely the end of his national coaching days but not the end of his career. He was destined for greater things— most likely at club level and almost inevitably overseas.

***

In the stands, Soccer Australia Chairman Kimon Taliadoros looked pensive and resigned to the game's fate. Everything he and his team had worked so hard for had disappeared in 90 minutes. So had the USD $14 million that the Federation would have received from FIFA for qualifying, money that many of his colleagues had already mentally banked.

Through the lens of a former player, Taliadoros saw the issues. Inwardly, he also had concerns as to how the Socceroos would adapt to Postecoglou's style when it mattered, but in reality, New Zealand were a well-organised, disciplined team and in many cases, man for man more talented than their Australian counterparts.

The Kiwis had their best team in over 30 years. Under the guidance of Dutch coach Pim Verbeek, who had form managing Asian countries and would now be a master stroke in navigating their upcoming AFC playoff, a combination of players with European and local experience had been melded into a tight-knit formidable squad. A no-nonsense defensive unit led by Winston Reid was merely the supporting act for their brilliant attacking midfield combination of Marco Rojas and Kosta Barbarouses. Up front, Chris Wood had wreaked goal havoc throughout qualifying and additionally now had two goals against Australia under his belt.

How had it come to this? Kimon grasped the reality that reforming Oceania for the better had led to a confederation-wide boon and it wasn't just for Australia's benefit. If Soccer Australia wanted a legitimate football region recognised and respected on the world stage, that meant raising playing standards as well as administrative reform right across the Pacific. It meant more serious competition, a levelling of the playing field as it were, and ironically greater financial risk for his Federation.

However, Taliadoros knew there was a greater irony at play, that lay in the reformed and now successful National Soccer League. And particularly, that lay in the hands of a wily Russian emigrant who spent much of his time on a beautiful rural property just outside of Christchurch.

When Slava Meyn executed his long-planned-for move of he and his family to New Zealand, he set about recreating his beloved Nakhodka FC, Shaky Isles style. He had every intention of settling around Auckland, but, on visiting the South Island, he fell in love with the Canterbury district and put down his new roots there. It wasn't long before he had formed an allegiance with the local football community and began to apply the very principles of club development and capital works investment that he had shared with the NSL's masters. Before long, Christchurch United had a 10,000 all-seater modular stadium and a youth academy the envy of Australasia. Local community loyalty followed, including healthy cross promotion with the neighbours down the road, Super Rugby's Crusaders.

Indignity and pushback came from the North Island and particularly New Zealand Football, who traditionally regarded Auckland as the powerhouse of the local game. But as Christchurch United began to sweep all before them domestically, it was inevitable that the local Federation would embrace the upstarts from the south. They made use of the club's impressive facilities and recognised that an increasing number of national player selections were coming from there.

In due course, the NSL made good on its arrangement with Meyn back in 2004 and Christchurch United entered the league in 2010. Within two seasons the club made its first finals series and was shoring up its local market across their country, with occasional home games at Wellington's 'Cake Tin' and Auckland's North Harbour Stadium scattered throughout the regular season.

Kimon gazed across the pitch at the celebrating Kiwis. The inspiration for and ultimate success of the NSL in creating a league based around broad geographical reach, community representation, active crowd support and boutique stadia had come back to bite the nation at an international level.

For the good of the game, thought Taliadoros with a wry smile to himself as he reflected on FIFA's motto.

Chapter 22

Sydney, Australia,

April 2015

The meeting formally concluded and Michael Darvos' colleagues surrounded him, offering their congratulations. It had been a unanimous decision that he succeed Remo Nogarotto as the Chairman of the Association of Professional Soccer Clubs.

Nogarotto had successfully guided the association for the last 12 years, with the implementation of the revitalised NSL, league expansion and the National Stadium Project all occurring under his watch. He had decided that he had achieved all that he could with both his club Northern Spirit and in his role in the APSC.

More time in Italy beckoned and it was time to move on, particularly when there was such an able replacement. He had been mentoring Michael Darvos for some time and saw much of himself in the younger man.

Darvos had been a Sydney Olympic fan as long as he could remember. He was fortunate enough at a formative age to witness the club's fabulous squads of the 1980s. As a fan on the sidelines and through his compulsive watching of SBS' *The World Game*, young Michael was convinced not only of football's status as the greatest game on the planet, but that the local form of the game was of a high standard and could achieve even greater things.

He had played as a junior, but academic study beckoned. A degree majoring in sports management—then just a fledgling subject—was followed by a business Master's degree. What began as a part-time role in Sydney Olympic's administration, juggled with a 'real' job, became a dream opportunity when he was appointed CEO of the club in 2010.

The timing aligned with Olympic's second grand final win in as many seasons. He had inherited a club much on the rise both on and off the park, and had since overseen the completion of the now all-seater St George Stadium.

And had been instrumental in helping establish the Australian Football Museum, in no small way because his club had the honour of housing it.

He was the perfect choice to replace Nogarotto.

***

Two weeks later, Darvos' dream appointment felt more like a poisoned chalice.

The weekend had started well enough, but by late Sunday afternoon worrying reports had begun to filter through. A hurried late night teleconference of the APSC had followed and now, the next morning, Michael felt like a truck had hit him. As he readied himself for the formal media conference, he again glanced through the morning newspaper's reports.

The Daily Telegraph had been, as usual, consistent with its familiar indignant tone towards soccer, barely disguising its bias and in turn undertaking any angle that would assist its all-but-contracted alignment with rugby league.

"This morning soccer faces up to yet another evil blemish on its copybook. Flares, fights involving up to 50 individuals, 12 arrests and three people admitted to hospital with stab wounds all occurred at what is meant to be a recreational pastime.

The trouble began yesterday afternoon during the game itself, but at the final whistle an all-in brawl resulted in the stands which then spilt to outside the ground. Police were called to break up the melee but not before a litany of assaults and injuries had occurred.

The Telegraph sought Police Commissioner Smith for comment. 'This kind of violence is unacceptable in Australia and will not be tolerated', he said. 'Unfortunately, it continues a long history of trouble at soccer matches. My concern is that the sport has some significant failings in the way it is managed and what's more, the game itself fosters these kinds of incidents. NSW Police will of course be conducting a full investigation.'"

Fairfax's Michael Cockerill had at least tried to give some context. *"No one can justify what happened yesterday, but we have to keep the role of the sport and the league in context for all of this. I have it on good authority that gang elements with nothing to do with the visiting side club or its supporters 'infiltrated' the away end of the ground with the intent of causing trouble with their rivals. How they got in and the management of their own fans' actions will and should be part of any investigation into the club. Sanctions will be forthcoming but please, can the authorities and the general public please understand, this is not about football per se."*

In *The Australian*, Ray Gatt had shown his frustration at both the impact upon the game he loved combined with a lack of any permanent corrective action.

"I have watched and reported on soccer for more than 40 years. For many reasons, I more than most understand the history of football in this country and those who fostered and developed our great game here. But nothing excuses the trouble what we saw yesterday and which surfaces from time to time. It is no excuse that this is just a small minority of fans or that somehow clubs and administrators are powerless. Something simply has to be done, if for no other reason than to save soccer from itself."

As expected, Andrew Bolt hadn't held back.

"So, what are we to make of this disgraceful organised violence? Others may be too politically correct to call it out for what it is. But I'm not. This is the modern-day outplaying of European tribal hostility that belongs in another century and on another continent. It has no place in contemporary Australia whose citizens have naively and with good will opened their land and their values to these people and their descendants. This kind of brazen gang-like activity represents a failure of not only the sport of soccer that fosters it, but of multiculturalism itself."

Darvos put the newspaper reports aside. He was furious with the louts who had instigated this, but also flustered that one or two of the association's clubs had failed to more actively manage what had been a recurring issue, bubbling just below the surface. This was despite the fact that the APSC had, overall, a good working relationship with the fan groups across the country.

In many ways, however, he was just as frustrated with the preconceived notions that both the press and the public had with respect to 'soccer violence'. In particular, that somehow the infrequency of scoring somehow bred so much frustration in the terraces that fans began fighting to keep themselves entertained. And by extension, through rule changes and 'making the goals bigger', the problems would magically disappear!

Or that the problems were alcohol fuelled. Whilst he inwardly felt a degree of *schadenfreude* when football fans posted 'whataboutism-style' videos of drunken fighting at AFL and cricket, he knew that there were different forces at work when it came to football.

The problem couldn't just be blamed on 'ethnicity'. Certainly some groups shared a common heritage and aligned themselves with the club founded by their forebears, but there was plenty of evidence that the football itself was only peripheral to their inappropriate behaviour. Besides, over the years skirmishes had occurred on the terraces of both 'traditional' and 'community based' clubs.

Michael knew there were different issues at play.

In short, Darvos knew that unfortunately, there was an antisocial, almost exclusively male, element that was attracted to football attendance. It was something about the way that supporting a football club, particularly for active fan groups, created a sense of bonding and shared passion at an emotionally charged level. Additionally, there was the attraction of a 'uniform', signing and chanting, protest, and the taste of either common victory or shared defeat, the latter often tied to some kind of injustice in a referee's decision or the opposing team's actions.

Sadly, there were some who found being part of active support was more like being part of a gang, with shared inappropriate values, 'territory' to be defended, and an opportunity to collectively challenge rules and law.

There would be recriminations, stern words within the association, attendance bans, further newspaper columns written. Probably more definitive action from Soccer Australia, who had the ultimate say with respect to disciplinary action.

Darvos honestly didn't know where to start, but there had to be a more permanent solution. And he needed to focus on the positives. Yesterday's events were unacceptable, but just this season alone, nearly two million people across the country had attended NSL games and enjoyed the experience. There'd been so much success over the last decade, that success would—*had to*—continue.

Michael sighed, rose and headed downstairs where the press eagerly awaited him.

Chapter 23

Darwin, Australia,

April 2016

It was warm and bright, the flies more overbearing than the heat. Nonetheless, Craig Foster was disappointed that the entourage of which he was part was directed inside the air-conditioned offices of the Harry Williams Institute. He would have much preferred to stay on the pitch with the local youngsters.

After all, the enthusiasm of the kids was infectious, as were their beautiful smiles. They scampered around kicking footballs under the watchful eye of the local coaches, who had been trained to ensure that every participant not only enjoyed themselves but learnt the basic skills of the game. They were of course also watching carefully for signs of blossoming talent.

Most importantly, there were girls as well as boys.

Once reluctantly inside, Foster and the rest of the six-person contingent were invited to take a seat and offered a glass of cold water. The head coach at the Institute, Doug Rivers of the local Larrakia nation, addressed them.

"Friends, thank you for visiting today and taking part in the formal opening ceremony. As you know, our Institute is named after a member of the 1974 Socceroos team and the first Indigenous player to grace the stage of the World Cup."

He paused, then continued. "The Williams Institute has three primary aims. Firstly, we want to play an important role in the local communities here around Darwin, as part of a multi-layered plan to engage Indigenous kids in both sport and education. Secondly, like many other Academies around the country, we want kids to learn the game of football and its skills in line with the Warren national curriculum. Thirdly, we want to identify and develop those talented gifted players who can graduate to the ranks of the NSL and perhaps also the Socceroos or Matildas!"

And fourthly, thought Foster, *this place does the best it can to stop other codes from getting their hands on them …*

More importantly though, he knew this centre's greatest strength was that it was planned, completed and now run by local First Nations people. *Give them the capability and they will deliver* was one of his mantras.

Watching the kids through the window, Foster thought back to his own progression through football. Born and raised in Lismore in northern New South Wales, his football prowess was rewarded with a move to Sydney Croatia in his late teens. Further Australian club soccer ensued before a stint in Hong Kong. On returning to Australia, he won both national selection for the senior team and a full-time professional career in England in the late 1990s. That phase of his journey was of course capped off with a pivotal role in Australia's greatest ever World Cup performance in *France '98*.

Perhaps it was the extent of his football travels, or maybe how his Anglo-Celtic upbringing in a regional town contrasted so starkly with his first experiences of multiculturalism at Sydney Croatia. But as he progressed from player to SBS commentator, his views on multiculturalism and Australian football's place in that movement gradually grew.

Now he was Soccer Australia's special envoy for diversity in football, but he was also an important liaison with the APSC with respect to talent development. It sat well with him but, as far as he was concerned, the agenda needed to continue to broaden. His mentor Johnny Warren had done much to bridge the traditional gap between the old 'white' Australia and post-war migrants.

Now there was a new century with new arrivals to Australia from Asia, Africa and the Middle East in particular. Australian football could be elevated to whole new heights if this could be tapped into. But Foster was thinking beyond that as well. *This country has so much entrenched racism and a terrible attitude to people seeking to make Australia home,* he had often articulated. *Something has to be done about it and someone has to speak up for them.*

Foster already had runs on the board. Five years ago, he had convinced Prime Minister Gillard to invest $25 million into a football-based integration program for asylum seekers as the government, at long last, had wound down offshore refugee detention centres. The stipend had been widely used by Soccer Australia in both training facilities that additionally assisted club football, as well as in human resources for skills development and coaching.

Now he was moving to the next level again, lobbying government for further investment as he formally positioned soccer as the game that endorsed and embraced diversity and inclusiveness, irrespective of background or birthplace. He had succeeded in emboldening football to speak up for itself, not to be afraid of its roots or its values in both boardrooms and before politicians. Just as importantly, he had helped give Australian soccer its cultural purpose.

The pleasantries completed, the contingent stepped back outside and having spotted them, the kids again sprinted over to greet the visitors. Foster enjoyed the attention. However, there was one famous player in the group the youngsters *really* wanted to see and meet, and that was, of course, Socceroo hero Adam Goodes.

***

Inspired by the 1997 World Cup qualification and prompted by his family, Adam Goodes had quietly withdrawn from the AFL draft held shortly after and returned to his childhood love of soccer. He played briefly for Adelaide City, where he had grown up, before being spotted by a Crystal Palace scout.

That led to a successful five-year career in the English Premier League as a right winger with a fearful whipped cross in from the by-line. He was seen as a natural balance for Stan Lazaridis, who plied his trade on the other side, and a very fitting replacement for retiring Socceroo Robbie Slater. It wasn't long before the national team setup came calling. Goodes had made his Socceroo debut in late 2000 at Craven Cottage in London in a friendly against Denmark, scoring from a 25-metre screamer into the top left of the goal and earning an assist from a cleverly crafted dipping and swinging signature cross for John Aloisi to put home on the volley.

Despite the widespread disappointment of 2002 qualification failure, Goodes enjoyed the ultimate career accolade by featuring at the 2006 and 2010 World Cups with distinction. He played 58 times for Australia, netting 15 goals. An international farewell friendly against Chile only the year before in Sydney had packed Homebush Stadium and was watched by millions across the country.

On the domestic front, a longing for Australia and a desire to return home saw a transfer to Sydney Olympic in 2009, where he helped spearhead the club's back-to-back league and grand final victories. He was a crowd favourite wherever he played, loved by Olympic fans, and respected and applauded across the country for his attacking style of play and his approach to life.

At some point during the high point of his career, Melbourne's *Herald Sun* had stumbled across his AFL draft nomination and ran an article with a headline 'Just how Goode would he have been at AFL?'

Soccer fans laughed out loud, but across the country, possibly even also behind the closed doors of AFL headquarters, there was a recognition that 'real' football had the capacity to offer sports people like Adam Goodes true international fame, the opportunity to represent your country at the highest level, the greatest self-satisfaction and quite frankly, the best pay packet.

Now here he was, progressively developing the emerging important responsibility for the rest of his life. At Olympic he was feted as their greatest Indigenous player since Charlie Perkins, and he recognised inwardly the magnitude of the task required for him to emulate Perkins' advocacy off the pitch.

Just as Craig Foster was reaching into the new emigrant and refugee space, Goodes' time to truly shine as an ambassador for Indigenous people, not only in football but across the whole of the country, had come.

He dribbled a ball across the manicured brown grass, with a string of kids chasing gleefully behind him.

Chapter 24

Sydney, Australia,

December 2016

Mark and Alanna Bowman, decorated with their red, white and yellow scarves, alighted from the Macquarie University Metro Station and commenced the short walk through the campus grounds to Spirit Stadium. Mark was never sure to what degree his now 22-year-old daughter came to the occasional football match just to humour her father and how much she enjoyed it. Certainly, it was a chance to catch up socially, as they hadn't lived under the same roof for years. In fact, Alanna had spent time away in Bathurst and even overseas completing her university education. But they always had fun, both at NSL games and at crucial World Cup qualifiers out at Homebush, even if they weren't religious weekly attenders.

And after all, there was serious history. Along with the rest of the family they had sat in the Bob Stand all those years ago in Northern Spirit's first season at North Sydney Oval. The half-innocent active supporters' most common chant was (clap, clap, clap clap clap; clap clap clap clap): "SPIRIT!!" and as the word was uttered, Alanna, then just a tiny tot, would touch her finger on Mark's nose with a smile. They still laughed about it, along with Mark's explanation to his young family that the crowd was at times suggesting that the referee was a *banker*.

These days, Alanna spent more time giving her perspective of the relative advertising and marketing strengths of the various football codes in Australia. Having recently started work as a media buyer, she now had insight as to her various clients' investments in sports broadcasting. There was the occasional wind-up of her father who regularly whinged about rival codes and the way they leveraged the market and the media, but she also knew full well the response she would get from him.

During college, she had run a few sports investment ideas for a project past her father and got an hour-long diatribe as to the evils of AFL for her efforts. It wasn't just the rubbish nature of the game itself, Mark would opine, it was the aggressive way they would use public money to shut out and put down other codes at grassroots level; the building of overlarge concrete bowls useless for real football, all on taxpayer's money; and above all, the very essence of sport was to represent your country, something that the ridiculous sport of AFL could not only never achieve but had effectively created a talent drain for aspiring Australia-representing athletes in a relatively small population nation.

Just think, Australia would have had significantly more Olympic medals and would already have been world champions at soccer and more times at rugby union, if it wasn't for that daft game! *Et cetera et cetera ...*

When all was said and done, Mark was a passionate hard-core fan of the world game. Like many north of the harbour, he had played as a youngster, but the professional circles he moved in his work life preferred rugby union and the entrenched code of Sydney had remained rugby league. Why, then, was Mark such a champion of the round ball code?

It was fundamentally his father's fault, who remained to this day a passionate fan and had instilled the same into Mark and his brothers. It was, after all, a great game to play and despite many matches being dour, on its day a football match could brilliantly and emotionally transcend any other spectator sport. There also was, of course, the repeated enticing struggle and ultimate failure of World Cup qualification after 1974 until 1997.

Above all, the dominance of football on a world scale appealed greatly to Mark. It was truly the game of the planet, yet for the first two decades of the NSL, he never had a settled club that he could feel connected to, and for all that time Australia had stood on the World Cup sidelines.

That combination had led to a noisy activism that had found its way into joining forces with an emerging online community and connecting in the stands with the faithful for those 'life or death' World Cup fixtures—but he was highly embarrassing to his wife at dinner parties.

Mark and Alanna's 15-minute walk brought them to just outside the ground, where they stopped to buy some dinner from one of the many pop-up tent stalls that were regular Friday night Northern Spirit fixtures. Luckily the shortest queues were for gozleme, their favourite. The local punters and the visiting Canberra fans seemed more intent on chicken satay sticks.

The fixture was a popular one for visiting Canberra United supporters. Despite the three-hour drive, many commented that there were only two sets of traffic lights between Viking Park and Spirit Stadium but several service centres along the way to keep them fed, even before they got to the chicken satay line. Many then made a weekend of it in Sydney, visiting friends and family or catching other sporting events over the next couple of days.

The Bowmans took their seats on the 18-metre line on the western side of the ground, just as the WNSL fixture was winding up. Spirit were trailing 3–1, and there had been much talk of late as to why the club that had literally tens of thousands of young women playing in their catchment area weren't doing better. Doubtless, more terse discussions were being had behind the closed doors of Northern Spirit's administration.

Beer in hand, Mark gazed around Spirit Stadium with a mixture of pride and satisfaction. Neither emotion could be directly attributable to anything he had done; in fact, in his only brief foray into the labyrinth of soccer politics many years ago he and his colleagues had failed to achieve their plans to rejuvenate the code. *No matter*, he thought. *Others achieved it anyway and who knows, they likely achieved a better outcome.*

Rather, Mark's emotions were on behalf of the sport itself and how, despite all the odds, soccer had become stable, sustainable and relatively popular. The game was still over-administered and could trip itself up in spectacular ways at a moment's notice, but there was unity in the game from grassroots juniors to elite international level. Off the field, the game's forays into the Indigenous space and in defending refugee rights meant that it stood for something.

Furthermore, football was the true embracer of multiculturalism and could count decades of credibility in that realm, with a rich history of clubs, some now well over half a century old, that began as various emigrant groups' social gatherings in an alien Australian landscape. Now they were community-representing outfits that had graced themselves on the international stage, at tournaments like the FIFA Club World Championship.

Crowds had increased modestly over the years and a 10,000 strong average was the accepted key performance indicator, it seemed. Many clubs had taken advantage of their stadium's modular design and added more seats over the last five years. Northern Spirit FC had already added a second tier over where Mark and Alanna now sat, and the behind-goal areas had also been expanded to now accommodate a stadium capacity of 15,000. As the men's kick-off loomed, it looked as if tonight's attendance might go close.

"Looking forward to a great game of soccer tonight!" said an anonymous voice behind Mark and to his right.

"You mean football!" came a reply from someone at random from close by.

Mark smiled to himself and preferred not to look around. He had spent his entire adult life in that lexical conundrum and frankly, was over the whole debate as a starter of arguments. Personally, he preferred the word football, partly on principle and worldwide usage, but mostly because it irked him that AFL would use every means possible to 'own' the word.

However, after years of agitation and indignation, there were now many times when for the purposes of explanation or mere conversational simplicity, it was just easier to say *soccer* and he no longer squirmed when he uttered the word. *Just don't tell my father that!* he thought with a grin.

With 15 minutes to go before kick-off and the majority of the crowd settled into their seats, the Phantoms made their way loudly into the Bush End.

With more than one eye on the Spirit name and just a touch of flair in some of their outfits, the active supporters of the northern Sydney club were amongst the most noisy and colourful in the league. Their tifos relied heavily upon the Graphic Arts and Marketing faculties of the nearby university who actively fostered the design and construction of the banners and further, happily stored them on campus for the group. One post-doc Fellow was even completing a Master's treatise into the social and cultural interplay of messaging at football matches.

In turn, the 'Skull Cave' or simply 'The Cave', as the active groups' bays were known, was full of a cross section of high school students, university undergraduates from diverse backgrounds, young, more traditional middle-class graduates and tradies.

This evening, one of their favourite tifos was hoisted as the teams entered the arena. It featured an oversize graphic of the famous comic book *Phantom*, his costume in team colours, with his arms crossed and adjacent to the message THE GHOST WHO SCORES!

The game kicked off and, after an initial settling-in period, Northern Spirit progressively gained the ascendancy. In defence that were a far more balanced outfit than the prior season, with the recently returned Connor O'Toole at left back and Rhyan Grant now cementing himself on the opposite side of the defence. Necevski as ever was solid between the posts and the latest marquee signing was working well alongside Alex Brosque up front.

On the Canberra side, coach Andy Bernal was gradually making his mark in assembling a squad that not only demonstrated talent but adhered to his no-nonsense policy of proven measured athleticism as the deal breaker for any professional footballer. James Troisi and Trent Buhagiar were combining well in attack and Bernal was starting to leverage the club's proximity to the Australian Institute of Sport as a source of young talent. He looked to have picked up an emerging gem in the young Kye Rowles.

Nonetheless, Spirit maintained their dominance and goals on either side of half time were a fair reflection of the difference in quality, on a true surface that allowed for accurate control, passing and generally a game of high standard.

The match entered injury time, and, with a two-goal buffer, it was clear that the points were staying home. The crew behind the goal kept their level of noise up and were rewarded at full time with the home team celebrating with them in a unified display between the terraces and the pitch.

Mark clapped his hands as the team and The Cave went through their celebrations.

He sat back, smiling. He realised that, at long last, Australian football had given him not only his simple wish for a team to support, but far more than that. From his early days behind the goal at Socceroo games in the '80s, to the famous Iran game in 1997 and following the national team through France the next year, to now a number of World Cup appearances and just simply with a regular club team to support, Mark had recognised that he couldn't really ask any more of the Australian version of the game he loved. From now on, he could be the contented fan in the stands, happy or upset by full time but also knowing there would be another fixture, another campaign in due course.

It was time for others to keep fighting the fight and argue the case, for the continued good of the game.

Mark turned to Alanna with a smile. "Should we head off, then?"

Chapter 25

Sydney, Australia,

April 2017

Michael Darvos gazed out over the lush turf at St George Stadium. As the CEO of Sydney Olympic, his office high up in the Raskopolous Stand gave him sweeping views of the entire pitch. The ground staff were at full tilt, preparing for Saturday's game against South Melbourne.

It was a magnificent sight, and, on the weekend, the European-style tiered stands would be full to overflowing. They could have sold out the 25,000-capacity stadium twice over, such was the popularity of the Big Blue. No matter. The game was live on national free-to-air television and via various platforms on NSL-TV, and Darvos knew that limited availability bred even more interest. Ratings were solid, even in a competitive world where the NRL and AFL had games on the same day and the nation more generally was preparing for Australia Unity Day festivities.

The National Stadium Strategy had been one of his predecessor's greatest triumphs. All cities across the country now had rectangular football grounds with seated capacity for 10 to 30,000 patrons attending NSL fixtures. Some were shared with the NRL or rugby union, but the majority were football owned or for exclusive use. The pitches were high standard and as a result, so was the match quality, not only for the NSL, but for the WNSL and especially the youth leagues.

Michael audibly sighed. It was all such a long way from Pratten Park in the '80s, where he had stood with his father around the oval picket fence.

Or was it?

The football had been a high standard—years ahead of its time in Australia—but what was lacking was the organisation, the will for tough decisions, the investment and quite frankly, the *governance*. He chuckled to himself. *You're starting to sound like you're back in your MBA classes, you malaka.*

He'd done his best to summarise the state of the game at the NSL's 40th anniversary dinner a few nights before in Melbourne. It was a gala affair and as Chair of the Association of Professional Soccer Clubs, Michael had star billing with a keynote speech to boot. He turned from the wonderful vista and walked back to his desk, picking up the speech and re-reading key parts of it to himself.

Ladies and gentlemen, we gather tonight to celebrate the oldest and most diverse national sporting competition in Australia. A league—and indeed, a game—that represents the true development of Australian society over decades and now also seeks to represent the tens of thousands of years from before European settlement. A league that today covers the entire geography of Australia and even stretches to New Zealand.

A league that whilst visionary at the outset, took over half of its life to truly establish itself. As you know, ladies and gentlemen, the best football minds in this nation, with the best will, could without significant change only operate successfully for so long. At the turn of the century, we nearly lost everything, with crowds, organisation, and bank balances in free fall.

If at that time the clubs were struggling to see the best way forward, government certainly had provided something of a blueprint to work with. From there, a new strategy, new firm will and investment, particularly in our own real estate, did the rest. The Association of Professional Soccer Clubs was born, fashioning itself somewhat in the image of the English Premier League. The national league was reborn and frankly, hasn't looked back since.

Michael scanned down the page.

… reform to the Federation has, I would argue, followed rather than led that of the NSL, but our association is grateful for the whole-of-game strides that Soccer Australia have implemented over the last decade. We remain committed to our role within the game, in particular managing the professional game and its future participants.

We continue to look forward. On the field, our 16 team men's league is now fully rounded out. Our national youth leagues continue to provide the best in future talent, and we commit to our continued development of the Women's NSL.

We pride ourselves in the way we have marketed and sold our product beyond the grandstands. We were early innovators in using online activity and social media to connect and engage our fans. We have fostered and grown our long-running association with SBS Television and are proud to have them as our free-to-air broadcast partners. In the pay-for-view television space, our initial production through cable television has evolved into internet subscription services. We are examining new ways of using online platforms for presenting games at various levels. There is a revolution about to take sport, especially football, worldwide by storm and once again, we want to be early adopters in this space.

We embrace Soccer Australia's move to launch a national second division next season and look forward to linking the two leagues in ways that can enhance all participating clubs and both competitions.

Darvos skipped forward to the closing part of the speech.

Ladies and gentlemen, we have found our place in the Australian sporting landscape. We understand the competitive nature of football codes in this country, but we choose to run our own race. We have led in the areas of multiculturalism, diversity, Indigenous participation and fan engagement. We are the only sport to have a true national women's league. We remain the most popular participation sport in the country and the only sport that has nationwide support each time the World Cup and Olympic Games come round.

We have the most vibrant, inclusive, financially stable—and by far the oldest—national sporting competition in the nation.

Ladies and gentlemen—I give you the National Soccer League—40 years young!"

Michael put the speech down. Of course, he knew that it wasn't all beer and skittles. Mainstream media still had it in for the game, with limited reporting in the popular press, unless there was a crowd skirmish—of course.

Thank God for the fan engagement scheme and the younger generation's uncanny ability to connect, organise and provide commentary, without ever reading a newspaper or watching a broadcast news bulletin. He said a quiet *thank you* to the APSC's promotions people for recognising these issues and implementing policy years before other codes did.

There were still issues with some grounds, and the challenge of bringing some up to standard in the event of formal promotion and relegation ever coming to pass. The Player's Association always wanted salary increases. And keeping sponsors happy was a constant chore—*heaven help us if we ever lose Virgin Airlines ...*

And then there was the national team's setup and the limitations of Australia's position in the football world, both geographically and politically. International breaks, FIFA statutes around national representation and better Australian medical protocols had advanced significantly over the last few years. Collectively they helped reduce the tyranny of distance, but the fact remained that Australian national teams, whilst ever a part of Oceania, had to ensure long periods of time deprived of serious international competition.

But to the APSC, did any of this matter? Did these challenges impede progress at the national league level, or was that concept irrelevant? There were competing arguments, but long ago, Michael and his association realised that the ongoing fostering of mainstream interest in the NSL could not simply hang off the performances of the country's various international teams.

And as for the Australia–NZ World Cup bid for 2026?? Well, let's see how that goes …

Darvos refocused. His mission was the national leagues, regardless of what happened to the Socceroos and Matildas. They were the Federation's problem. He returned his thoughts to the NSL and looked up at the Sydney Olympic logo on his office wall.

Momentarily, he wondered what would have happened if the National Soccer League had failed in 2003.

The game would have survived, he thought. *It always does.* Probably someone would have started another national league. After all, the Americans did it. He closed his eyes and, *déjà vu* like, he could visualise a different Australian league, with franchised teams like those in America's Major League Soccer, including a team just like his based in Sydney, playing in blue … uncannily, it seemed so close and real.

Nonsense! he thought. He opened his eyes and looked again at the ground and towards the Katholos Stand where the active fans would be on Saturday. Thousands of them, singing, waving countless scarves and flags, and doubtless hoisting an enormous tifo adorned by their favoured logo of the Sydney Harbour Bridge decorated with the Olympic rings.

Now *that's* the reality.

The Sliding Doors Timeline

1997–2017

Nov 1997	Australia defeats Iran and qualifies for *France 1998*.
Jul 1998	Australia defeated by Argentina in World Cup Quarter Final.
	Australian coach Terry Venables departs.
Jul 1999	Frank Farina appointed Socceroos coach.
Nov 2000	Northern Spirit consider moving from North Sydney Oval.
Nov 2001	Australia defeated by Paraguay in two-legged COMNEBOL/OFC playoff for *Korea–Japan 2002*.
Dec 2001	Australian coach Frank Farina sacked; Raul Blanco appointed interim coach.
Dec 2002	Crowds in free fall at NSL fixtures; predicted folding of NSL after the 2002/3 season.
Feb 2003	David Hill resigns as Soccer Australia Chairman; Board member Les Avory appointed new Chair.
May 2003	BKG Investment Group finalises corporate restructure of NSL. Association of Professional Football Clubs (APSC) formed, Remo Nogarotto appointed Chairman.

Sep 2003	New look 10 team NSL launched:
	Brisbane Lions, Newcastle, Northern Spirit, Sydney Olympic, Sydney Utd, Melbourne Knights, Melbourne City, South Melbourne, Adelaide Utd, Perth Glory.
Apr 2004	Northern Spirit commence three season tenure at Brookvale Oval.
May 2004	Plans for National Stadium Project finalised.
Aug 2004	Marconi rejoin and Canberra Utd join NSL for 2005/6 season, creating 12 team league.
Nov 2004	Bora Milutinovic appointed Socceroos coach in one year deal, pending World Cup qualification.
May 2005	Work commences at Knights Stadium, Lakeside and St George Stadium.
Jul 2005	Soccer Australia complete corporate restructure under CEO Stefan Kamasz.
	Soccer Australia and Oceania successfully negotiates OFC/AFC playoffs for 2006 and 2010 World Cups.
Aug 2005	Strategic plan initiated by Soccer Australia to investigate revamping of Oceania administration.
Oct 2005	Australia wins Oceania World Cup qualifying section.
Nov 2005	Australia defeats Bahrain in OFC/AFC playoff; qualifies for *Germany 2006*.
May 2006	Stadium development work commences at Marconi Stadium and Richlands.

Jun 2006	Australia reaches round of 16 at Germany 2006, defeated by Spain.
	Bora Milutinovic departs as Socceroos coach.
Jan 2008	Ange Postecoglou appointed Socceroos coach after the position is fallow for 18 months.
Sep 2008	West Sydney Rovers join and Brisbane Strikers rejoin NSL, creating 14 team league for 2008/9 season. WSR play out of Parramatta Stadium.
	Northern Spirit complete first phase of Spirit Stadium, move to new ground for 2008/9 season.
Oct 2008	Warren national curriculum implemented.
Nov 2008	Kimon Taliadoros replaces Les Avory as Soccer Australia Chairman, completes implementation of Oceania Confederation reforms.
May 2009	Redevelopment of Perry Park commences.
Nov 2009	Australia qualifies for *South Africa 2010*.
Mar 2010	Melbourne Football Stadium opens.
Jun 2010	Oceania negotiates all future World Cup qualifications via OFC/AFC playoff.
	Australia exit at group stage of *South Africa 2010*.
	Postecoglou stays on as Australian coach.
Sep 2010	Christchurch United and Southern Stars (representing Geelong and Launceston) join the NSL, creating a 16-team league for 2010/11 season. Southern Stars play at Geelong Stadium and (an upgraded) Northern Rangers Football Club ground.

Jun 2011	Plans finalised for Australian Football Museum located at St George Stadium.
Sep 2011	Australian Football Supporters Group gain formal membership position in Soccer Australia Congress.
Oct 2013	Australia eliminated by New Zealand in final OFC qualifying for *Brazil 2014*.
	Postecoglou sacked as Australian coach; Graham Arnold appointed.
May 2014	Additional level of seating added to Spirit Stadium.
Apr 2015	Sydney Olympic CEO Michael Darvos replaces Remo Nogarotto as APSC Chairman.
Feb 2016	Michael Darvos' report into fan engagement and stadium security titled *A Great Day Out* is released.
Apr 2016	Harry Williams Institute opens in Darwin.
Apr 2017	40th anniversary of the NSL.

ACKNOWLEDGEMENTS

Behind my brainstorming of highly fictional scenarios that have never happened, this work required a significant amount of research, particularly in the early chapters to keep some historic continuity with the real world. I have also relied on the thoughts and expertise of many, either directly through conversation or indirectly through their writings or public statements. I am grateful for their input, even if they didn't realise that they were contributing to the content of this book!

This work comes after a long medical career whereby I had over decades developed a distinct technical writing style—succinct and fact-based, designed for scientific publications and medical conference presentations. My only other body of work of similar length to this was my doctoral thesis, so adapting to fiction was a challenge. As I have always enjoyed reading my friend Matthew Hall's writing and having derived much inspiration from his style, a special thank you goes out to him.

Having pitched the idea to write this book, I found myself suddenly in the world of writing and publishing. I'm grateful for the multiple insights and bits of advice I received from accomplished football fiction writer Texi Smith.

Perhaps the most successful strategy the fictional Association of Professional Soccer Clubs implemented was the 'National Stadium Project'—in fact, the basis for this exists in our world. Well before I started *The Yawning Giant*, the late Michael Cockerill wrote two important articles in *The Sydney Morning Herald* about the inflated cost of stadia building in Australia and he referred to the real-life

Slava Meyn, who was investigating modular stadium construction techniques in his adopted city of Christchurch. It's worth noting that the strategy of boutique purpose-built and appropriately sized stadia is now a popular one and not just in football.

I am grateful to the tireless and often unpaid effort that the small group of Australian football historians have put in over decades, to ensure that the rich history of our game endures. I would like to acknowledge the entire *OzFootball.net* crew and in particular Andrew Howe.

Their collected writings and statistics, including within Howe's *Encyclopedia of Socceroos* (also published by Fair Play Publishing), made it relatively easy for me to, for example, slot Australian representatives into fictional games or come up with squads for 21st century NSL teams that were in fact borrowed from contemporary real-life A League squads.

I had the honour of spending time with passionate fans like David McGaw and Todd Blackwell, without whom I couldn't have written the Newcastle chapter. That chapter also features a detailed discussion as to how a club community ownership model might succeed in Australia. The practical details came from discussions with Rubens Camejo who has thought and written extensively about this, as well as other structural problems with soccer in Australia. His blog is well worth a read.

I have now attended two editions of the Football Writers' Festival (created and developed by Fair Play Publishing) and had the pleasure of hearing various football luminaries speak about their lives and their philosophies. In writing about those individuals in this book, I hope that I have faithfully interpreted some of their thoughts and stories so that they might achieve even greater things in my imaginary world.

Thanks to Pablo Bateson who gave me a crash course in fan groups and advocacy in its various forms around the globe and how active support can be fostered and protected without either hooliganism or over-policing.

Finally, this work should be seen through the eyes of a football fan more than anything else. A far from naïve fan, but one who is not an administrator, an elite athlete, a journalist or a media personality. In the end, much of the inspiration put into these pages comes from ordinary yet passionate fans like those in my immediate family and the many characters I have stood or sat with in the terraces or communicated with over many decades. There are hundreds of thousands of us out there across the country who deserve better and need to be brought back to more actively support our beautiful game.

I can only make structural changes to Australian football in fiction; those of you who are running the sport are those who can do do something about it.

Please let this book be your inspiration.

Mark Bowman
February 2023

Follow @theyawninggiant on Twitter for ongoing news and views on the National Soccer League, now in its 46th year, and football in Oceania.

ABOUT THE AUTHOR

Mark Bowman has spent most of his adult life juggling a passion for football with a career as a medical specialist in the treatment of infertility, in particular IVF.

After watching the Socceroos qualify for their first World Cup in 1973 on TV with his father, he spent the next 32 years in torment watching repeated qualification failure every four years, usually from the terraces. In between those big-ticket games, there was little to cheer for internationally and domestically, and although he attended many National Soccer League matches, Mark had no true club to support apart from during the brief existence of Northern Spirit FC.

Despite Australian football's successes since 2005 on the world stage and at long last, a club team to support in Sydney FC, Mark has long dreamt about alternative outcomes for the game he loves and has often wondered what might have been, under different circumstances.

His late night musings, lateral thinking, love of both anecdotes and football culture more generally, finally came together in *The Yawning Giant*, which he is quite certain will be his only one and only novel.

MORE REALLY GOOD FOOTBALL FICTION FROM POPCORN PRESS

Jarrod Black
Chasing Pack

Anna Black
This girl can play!

The End of the Game

The Gaffer

Game

POPCORN
PRESS